ALL THE THINGS WE FOUND

RIVER VALLEY LOST & FOUND: BOOK TWO

KAYLA TIRRELL

for my husband, who will get all my Doctor Who references.

(which may or may not be a result of me forcing him to watch it with me...)

CHAPTER ONE

GWEN

DIMPLES WOULD BE the death of me.

Okay, probably not the actual death of me. Also, not just any dimples, but Mitch's dimples in particular. They were dangerous. Not just because they were mesmerizing—which they were—but also because they happened to be attached to my best friend.

My very male and very single best friend.

We sat together at the local coffee shop, Beans & Things, trying to stay warm. It was February in Idaho. The weather was ridiculously cold, and hot lattes always made me happy.

The shop had a whimsical feel to it that was in direct conflict with the weather outside. Instead of regular booths or tables, metal bistro sets painted different cheerful colors filled the space. Between the seating and the hanging plants that decorated the windows, it felt like a magical garden that happened to serve coffee. When I wasn't here with my other best friend, Katie, I could usually persuade Mitch to come with me.

Today he had been the one to invite me out. He said he

had some news he wanted to share. It didn't necessarily mean anything. Buying a new baseball cap was sometimes considered news to him. Regardless, when he wanted to get together, I usually came running. Especially if that meant a caffeine fix.

Mitch was a good looking guy. His dark hair was always styled in a way that made it appear that he had just rolled out of bed. I knew better. His green eyes always promised mischief. Unfortunately, it was his mouth that caused my brain to turn to literal mush.

Every. Single. Time.

As he talked, I couldn't keep my eyes from the two indentions on either side of his mouth. The way they moved with each word he spoke was fascinating. When he closed his lips together, they would deepen. Other words he spoke would make them disappear altogether. How was that even possible?

It didn't matter how much time I spent watching them, I was newly fascinated every time he moved his lips. They begged for attention I was unable to deny. So much so that I hadn't realized Mitch had finished speaking and was looking at me, expectantly waiting for a response to what he had been saying. "So, what do you think?"

"About which part?" I asked in an attempt to hide the fact I hadn't heard a word he said the last few minutes. With any luck, he'd changed subjects enough times he'd be compelled to say something that hinted toward what he was asking.

"My job, what do you think?" he answered a little impatiently, but not without his patented smile. That stupid smile that had its own way of affecting me.

I mentally shook my head to focus. "Um, I think the

club is great," I eventually answered slightly confused as to why he was asking me about his job.

Mitch worked at the local gun club. It was a place where you could go and shoot different targets. Most of the time, Mitch was stuck running the skeet machine while guys practiced their aim on moving objects. I knew he thought it was boring, but you took what you could get in River Valley. Jobs weren't always easy to come by in a small town.

"You weren't listening."

"Of course, I was listening. I just wanted to make sure I..." My voice trailed off, and I finally stopped, unsure of how I was going to cover for my daydreaming. "Fine! I wasn't listening. What about your job?"

"Well, I was just saying I don't work there anymore. I quit," he said with a proud smile on his face.

"You quit?" I shrieked. "Why would you do that?"

His smile fell, and he shook his head back and forth as he leaned back against the metal chair he was sitting in. "See? I knew you weren't going to respond well to it." He placed his hands on the edge of the table, tapping his fingers. His eyes were trained on the movement in an obvious attempt to avoid making eye contact with me.

"Mitch, of course I'm not going to respond well. There aren't a lot of jobs right now. Julian still hasn't found a new one, and it's been weeks since he was fired from the diner."

"Maybe that has more to do with the fact that he was fired than there not being any jobs available." Mitch shrugged his shoulders as he said this, still not meeting my eyes. "Besides, I have some money stashed away in my bank account. I'll be fine."

I'll be fine.

The words pissed me off. Mitch was one of my best

friends. We had become friends almost immediately after I moved here from California a few years ago. He was easy to get along with, but he was always so carefree about everything. I mean, truly to a fault.

Mitch lived life to the fullest without fear of anything bad happening. It was as if he embodied everything older people said about teenagers. *They think they're invincible. They never think something bad will happen to them.* Frustratingly, nothing bad ever did happen to him.

Yep. I was an awful friend for even thinking that.

I didn't actually want something to happen to him. It just seemed so unfair he could do whatever he wanted and never be dealt the consequences.

"What if something happens? That money would be gone before you could blink."

"Well, if it does, I'll cross that bridge when I get there. Honestly, Gwen, you are the biggest worrier I've ever met. I don't think there's a bigger Nervous Nellie than you."

"Nervous Nellie?"

"It's something my mom says sometimes. Seriously, you need to relax."

If only he knew. If only Mitch or any of my friends knew the demons that were lurking beneath the surface, hiding in my past. They would go running for the hills. Or, maybe they would understand why I couldn't do daring anymore, why my life was a series of calculated decisions. But I had chosen to leave my closest friends in the dark, living with my past in secrecy. I couldn't expect them to understand why I couldn't just relax.

I remembered reading an article online once about high-functioning anxiety. I wasn't even searching the term, didn't realize it was a thing. And yet, I ended up going through the list and thinking that I could identify with almost everything.

Checking my surroundings constantly? Of course. It's smart to be aware.

Showing up to things early? That's just common courtesy.

Not having a large circle of friends? I thought it was better to put my energy into the ones I cared about.

The list went on and on. Nothing necessarily harmful or destructive. However, when put together, I could see that I was the prime example. These were habits that I'd adopted over the last couple of years, milestones to being a grownup. Or so I thought. Now, because of that stupid article, I couldn't help but overanalyze every action. Was I responsible? Was I suffering from mental illness? It was infuriating.

I took a deep breath and answered Mitch who was growing impatient with my silence. "Fine, I'll bite. Why did you quit your job?"

"If you weren't over there daydreaming, you would know." His fingers stopped tapping as he studied my face. "I probably shouldn't tell you. You know, to punish you for being a bad friend and not paying attention."

His words made me laugh. Only he would claim I was subject to daydreaming. I wasn't normally so ditzy. In fact, most people found my attentiveness to be unsettling. But those stupid dimples made me, well, stupid. "Oh, my goodness, just tell me," I cried across the table.

"I was channeling my inner Gwen," he explained. "I think I'm going to go into business and wanted to give myself more time to study."

"And party?" I guessed, my voice flat.

"Well, of course. If something is going to suffer, it's not

going to be the fun stuff," he admitted, his smile returning to his face.

"Of course not," I muttered under my breath, but I knew he heard me when I felt his foot kick me beneath the table.

Mitch and I had a weird relationship—one-part best friend, one-part sibling, and one-part romantic tension. All of that combined to make things really hard to decipher between us. It wasn't just on my end either. I knew that Mitch struggled with the same feelings that I did.

We just refused to talk about it.

"I know it's hard for you to see the value in anything fun. But we're only young once, Gwen. Shouldn't we be enjoying ourselves?"

"You mean like YOLO?"

"Please don't ever say that again, even ironically." He forced a dramatic shudder like I had made some unthinkable faux pas.

I rolled my eyes. "It's not that I don't value fun. I like to have fun like everyone else."

At this, he rose his brows at me. "Really?"

"Yes, really," I argued. I had fun all the time. I went tubing down the river when the weather was warmer. I liked building snowmen in the snow. Katie and I hung out and did girls' nights together. I was fun, damn it.

"Then how come all your fun always revolves around old lady activities?"

"I don't know what you're talking about," I said, conveniently leaving out the fact I had a how-to knit book sitting on my desk at home. I knew it was an old lady hobby, but didn't hipsters do it too? Were hipsters even a thing anymore?

"Then come to Brett Garlington's party this weekend with me," Mitch said, interrupting my internal debate.

"Isn't he in high school?"

"Yeah, but Sam's going, and I have big brother duties." His parents were so protective over Mitch's little sister, it wasn't funny. For some reason, they didn't think she was capable of making it through high school without a chaperone.

"I'm not going to be the college student who goes to a high school party," I argued.

"Why not?"

"Everyone will be younger than us. It'll be weird."

"Only if you make it weird. We could boss them around." He waggled his eyebrows at me.

I couldn't help but laugh at him. "You're horrible!"

He leaned forward in his seat. "Does that mean you'll come?"

"I don't know."

"Gwen, don't be ridiculous. It's only a party. What's the worst that could happen?"

I looked over at Mitch, his expression hopeful. I hated parties. The only good thing about Brett's party was it was a week away. I gave me time to mentally prepare, maybe even forget about it in the meantime.

I sighed. "Fine. I'll go."

CHAPTER TWO

MITCH

ON TUESDAYS, Gwen and I rode to school together. Truthfully, we drove to Boise State together most days. Tuesdays were the days it made the most sense since our schedules lined up almost perfectly. It had started with us taking turns making the drive to save money.

I also enjoyed having someone else in the car to keep me company during the commute. I thought that Gwen felt the same. It was almost an hour drive both ways. It could get lonely riding by yourself listening to the same songs every day.

Tuesdays were a nice break from the monotony.

But then Gwen realized that she could use some extra time in the campus library on Mondays after humanities. Her professor had the class do a lot of extra reading, so she started riding with me on that day too. This meant she could hang out for a couple of hours studying while I finished my own classes.

Then, it turned out, I needed some extra help in calculus, so I found a tutor who was willing to meet me early on Wednesday mornings. That way, Gwen and I could still ride together and get her to chemistry lab on time. Otherwise, it wouldn't have been worth the trouble of getting the extra help. I had no desire to take an extra trip if it wasn't beneficial for us both.

Thursdays were all over the place, but we couldn't resist half-off bagel day at a local bakery on the way to Boise, could we? We both loved getting our everything bagels smothered with cream cheese. We'd stuff our faces on the drive and spend the rest of the day trying to gross each other out with our breath. We would sneak up on each other in the halls, or the quad, or wherever we ended up crossing paths that day.

Gwen had been known to let out a few unladylike burps in an attempt to get me. For some reason, it just endeared her to me even more. Nothing like the smell of onion and garlic being blown in your face.

Fridays were our free day, a blessed extra day added to the weekend, so we didn't have to worry about the commute. Although, Gwen usually worked these days and we rarely saw each other.

But today was Tuesday, our official carpool day. I drove my truck through the snow knowing how much Gwen hated driving her car in this kind of weather. Having grown up in California, she didn't learn how to drive in the snow or have much experience looking for patches of black ice.

Between her lack of expertise and her cautious personality, I just assumed that we'd be taking my truck. I picked her up on our way without even texting. I'd never had this type of relationship before. The kind where you just knew what the other person wanted without having to ask. There was a level of comfort in that.

I looked over at her bundled up in the seat of my cab. She wore clothing from head to toe, the padding from her jacket and scarf hiding the figure I knew was under it. It was all topped off with a bright orange beanie.

Gwen was beautiful. Not in the usual way girls were hot. But in her own unique *Gwen* way. She didn't try to dress up or spend a lot of time in the bathroom getting ready. I liked that.

Okay, confession time: I knew she spent less time getting ready than I did. She was acting high maintenance if she brushed her hair, which was cut short. And I don't think she ever wore makeup.

She didn't need it.

My attraction to her wasn't a secret. I had on several occasions put myself out there. Every time I did, she would find a way to blow me off or change the subject. Or even worse, pretend like she didn't understand what I was saying or doing. That was the reaction I hated the most.

I had hit the point where I stopped throwing myself at her, but it didn't mean I had stopped holding onto hope for her to come around. I didn't like that I had a crush on my best friend. It killed me that she refused to acknowledge that she felt the same way because I knew she had feelings for me too.

I glanced over at her again. She was still rubbing her hands together even though we'd been in the truck for several minutes. "That hat is ridiculous," I said, yanking the misshapen beanie off her head, waiting to see what her reaction was.

Gwen's cheeks turned red as she tried to snatch it back from me. Her hands kept coming at me in a flurry of motion. "It's not that bad."

"It looks like it was knit by a blind woman with one hand."

"Mitch," she scolded me, never stopping her attempts to grab the monstrosity.

"That had horrible arthritis."

"Stop it." She punched my arm with one hand while still swinging the other wildly.

"Wait," I said when she refused to give up, realization dawning on me. "*You* made this, didn't you?" I laughed loudly. "Oh, this is great. Please let me wear it for the rest of the day."

She shook her head wildly.

"Come on, Gwen. When people give me strange looks, I'll just tell them I didn't have the heart to tell my girlfriend how bad it was."

"I'm not your girlfriend."

I couldn't help but notice *that* was the argument she made.

I put the hat on my head, even though it was way too small, ignoring her protests. I was happy it was orange and not something more girly like pink. Not that it would have stopped me though. "They won't know that."

"Just wait until I make the matching scarf. Then you'll be sorry," she laughed, leaning back against the seat giving up the fight. Her arms were crossed over her chest.

"I'll look like a giant tangerine."

"Poor Katie will feel like she's in Florida again surrounded by menacing citrus."

"Can citrus *be* menacing?"

Gwen lowered her voice to a deep growl. "I'll Vitamin C you in hell. Muah ha ha ha!"

"That was terrible," I told her, but neither one of us cared. We laughed at her pun as if it was the funniest thing we'd ever heard.

In fact, the two of us joked around back and forth the

entire drive before finally arriving at school. Once we got there, we went in our separate directions. For all our carpooling, we didn't have a single class together. I wasn't sure if it was due to us pursuing different majors or just wanting to take different things.

Regardless, I continued to wear the hat that Gwen had made. I got a few comments from some of my fellow students. A few people laughed knowing I was fully aware of how I looked with it on my head. There was no way to know everyone on campus, but the people who knew me knew that I was a goofball.

It made me smile knowing that Gwen had created it. I loved that she was unafraid to try new things, even if they were super dorky. If only she could take that bravery and apply it to all the areas of her life.

She'd be unstoppable.

Unfortunately, the girl was afraid of her own shadow. She'd try to play it cool, pretend like she was carefree. It only lasted for so long though. Eventually, the stress would get to her, and she'd snap like a rubber band. I took these opportunities to crack jokes and bring her out of it.

The day went by in a blur, my attention split between my classes and a certain girl who had no business knitting. Every time it made my head feel itchy throughout the day, I pictured her face when she had admitted to knitting it. I kept catching myself smiling. I couldn't wait to see her later.

My fingers tapped and knees bounced wildly through the last few minutes of class. My body was attempting to make time move faster. I was always filled with extra energy. Sitting still was my idea of hell. Even more so when I was looking forward to something.

"Let's go to a movie," I said when we were finally reunited. We always walked together to the parking lot. It never ceased to amaze me how in tune we were. How we didn't need to talk about how things would go, we just fell into step. Just like with me picking her up that morning.

We each had our place that fit perfectly with each other. Kind of like a puzzle piece if you wanted to get cheesy.

"Only if you promise not to wear that thing," she answered, nodding her chin in the direction of the hat she knitted. "It really is awful."

"Do you see how I look out for you? I took this to save you from the ridicule you surely would have gotten if you had worn it," I countered, but took it off as we got into my truck. We drove to the theater in Boise. River Valley was too small to have its own theater. By going to see something while we were already out here, I was saving us gas money. And matinee tickets were always cheaper anyway.

I was a pretty awesome friend to go through all the effort to save those extra dollars. There definitely wasn't any other motivation behind it.

None at all.

We went and saw some superhero movie. The latest in the long list of reboots and re-reboots. They were not my thing, not by a long-shot. But Gwen, she was a complete nerd. In the cutest way, of course. She loved all that geeky stuff.

I was a dude; I was supposed to like it, too. There had to be a code out there somewhere saying guys had to like action movies. I didn't. I went along with her so I could at least pretend I knew what I was talking about. And to spend more time with her.

It had been difficult to pay attention while we were watching the movie. I was distracted and found my eyes constantly moving over to check in with Gwen. She didn't seem to notice or care but kept her attention on the screen. The light from the screen lit her face up just enough to highlight her lips. I sat on my hands to keep myself from touching them.

I knew she would be pissed if I did it, especially in the movie theater. Not only would I be distracting her from the movie, but I would also be putting pressure on her that she wasn't ready for.

So I sat there trying to pay attention to the plot and to keep my eyes off of Gwen's face. I counted to fifty at least a hundred times and recited the pledge of allegiance just as many. I couldn't focus on the storyline. Going to movies together wasn't something foreign to us. I couldn't put my finger on why I was feeling so antsy this time.

I practically bolted when the move was done, even though I knew Gwen would want to watch until after the credits were finished. She liked to stay just in case there was some hidden Easter egg or some other inside joke that I wouldn't get.

To her credit, she didn't complain as she followed me and was being a good sport about my sudden mood until she saw that the snow had begun to fall harder while we were inside. Her steps slowed as we approached the windows of the building. I could see she was anxious. She hated anything with a perceived danger. I refused to let her dwell on it.

I grabbed her hand and pulled her through the front door of the theater, barely giving the people around us enough time to get out of our way. We started running through the parking lot while I loudly hummed the music from the movie we had just watched. It was a miracle I could even remember how it went considering how distracted I was the entire time.

I was jumping around like I was a superhero. I could hear her laughter as I dragged her behind me and knew I had been able to take her mind off of the weather at least for a few minutes. I loved when I could ease the constant anxiety she had bearing down on her.

When we got inside my car, I watched as she tried to wipe off the snow, all in different stages of melting, from her body gracefully. Her hair was slightly damp on the top and a stubborn snowflake stuck to her eyelashes.

I chose to shake my head back and forth like a dog, attempting to send water her way. Not that I was wet enough to get any on her.

"You are the worst," she yelled and playfully pushed me with both of her hands. She came at me full force. Unfortunately, with all my moving around, I wasn't prepared for it. We both went tumbling back into my seat, the top part of her body resting on mine. Our faces were just a couple inches apart.

I couldn't even begin to explain what happened next. The entire mood inside the cab changed in that moment. The air shifted, the electricity between us charged. Or maybe I imagined the whole thing because I had been strung so tightly for the past two hours.

Whatever it was, I knew that she felt it too. This was the moment I had been waiting for, the one I knew would eventually happen. One that couldn't be forced. It just had to happen naturally.

I was going to kiss Gwen.

She didn't hurry to move away but just looked up into my eyes with the same intensity I knew I was looking at her with. I brushed a few strands of her hair away from her face. They weren't long, but a couple of stubborn pieces caught in her eyelashes. The snowflake from mere moments ago had melted.

"Gwen," I said, not knowing how to express what I was feeling in that moment. How relieved I was to have her in my arms. My voice sounded rough to my ears. When had I started breathing so quickly?

Gwen's brows furrowed together as the hand I had just used to move hair out of her eyes was now cupping her face. My thumb traced her jaw as I leaned in slowly, reminding myself that this was Gwen. She spooked more easily than a deer.

I struggled to keep my breathing even, and I closed my eyes as my lips almost reached hers. So close I could feel the heat from her mouth against my own.

"I can't do this," Gwen said in a rush, her lips bumping mine as she spoke—not a kiss, but the briefest contact. Her body stiffened before jerking back from my touch.

I didn't open my eyes as I closed the fingers that had been touching her cheek into a loose fist. Not because I was angry, but because I had been so close and I was desperately trying to hold on to that moment.

I took a deep breath. "Gwen," I repeated her name, this time with much more desperation.

"I'm sorry," she whispered. I opened my eyes to see her shaking her head. "I'm sorry." She squeezed her eyes closed like she was in pain.

"Gwen, look at me," I said as I smiled as genuinely as I could, faking lightheartedness that wasn't there. She slowly opened her eyes while I reassured her it was fine.

It wasn't fine.

"Mitch."

"You know I get caught up in the moment sometimes. All that running around like a superhero just made me think I was supposed to kiss the damsel in distress." I nudged her playfully.

She gave a small laugh, a shadow of a laugh really, but managed to tease me back. "I was not the damsel in that scenario."

"No, I suppose you weren't," I replied before driving us home in awkward silence.

CHAPTER THREE

GWEN

I TEXTED Mitch that morning telling him that I needed to get to class even earlier than usual because of something to do with my chemistry lab. I apologized for not being able to ride together.

There wasn't anything extra I needed to do for chemistry, but I didn't think I could stand being in the car with him after what had almost happened. He had tried to kiss me. It was the most brazen he'd ever been with me. I needed some space to think about the way he had looked at me. To think about the way I had rejected him.

I was sure he saw right through the lie about carpooling, but he didn't call me out on it. I was thankful he let it slide. I loved that he knew when I needed space and didn't try to push me.

I wanted so badly for him to kiss me. I'd spent the previous evening obsessing over every detail trying to figure out why I didn't just let him. I touched my fingers to my lips, curious about what it would feel like to have his mouth against mine. Something more than the brief contact when I spoke. I could almost imagine what it would be like.

Frustration had me wanting to stomp my foot. I barely resisted the urge before leaving for class.

I went to class and did the bare minimum to make it through the assignment given to our group. After that, I bailed on psychology. I went straight home and asked Katie to come over. Thankfully, both of my parents were at work. They would have had lots of opinions about me ditching class and definitely wouldn't approve of me hanging out with Katie instead of pursuing my studies. As it was, they were more and more on edge lately.

I was too antsy to study or to sit through a class. I had so much anxious energy to burn that I could power the entire city of River Valley for a month. Maybe that wasn't saying a lot considering the size of our small town, but I needed to do something.

Usually, when I felt this way, Katie and I would go running. With the weather being in the 40s that day, there was no way I was going outside. Katie, having lived in Florida for several years, was just as wimpy as I was when it came to the cold weather. Actually, I thought she was worse than me, but I would never tell her that. We were both transplants trying to make it through the winter.

Instead of a long run around the neighborhood, we were going to do a workout video. Not just any video either, but an old DVD I found hiding in the back of the entertainment center. The guy on the cover wore the shortest shorts imaginable and wore a big grin on his face.

This was exactly what I needed.

Katie showed up in clothing that was way too cute to be worn for a workout, a pair of designer leggings with mesh cutouts and a top that had a bunch of crisscrossed fabric on the back of it. I looked down at the pajamas I had thrown on over my sports bra. I think I even spotted a mustard stain.

"What in the world is that?" my friend asked looking down at the case in my hand.

I shrugged nonchalantly, forcing my expression to stay neutral, even though I was howling inside.

"Gwen, I'm not doing that."

"Yes, you are," I argued giving her a sweet smile.

"I thought you were upset, which is why I agreed to come over and do this with you. I didn't realize you wanted to torture me."

"This isn't torture. It's therapy."

She looked skeptical. "It had better be therapeutic because I'm not sure I could do that and keep my street cred."

"I hate to break it to you, but you don't have any street cred."

"Obviously, it's residual from Julian," Katie argued.

"It doesn't work that way."

"Fine," she said. "Turn the stupid thing on." Her words might have been harsh, but her expression said otherwise.

Forty-five minutes later, having spent much more time making fun of the routine and not actually doing most of it, the guy on the screen was finishing up. Katie and I looked at each other and started laughing again.

The video had consisted of a great deal of clapping and walking in place. The songs that played were older than my parents, and I about lost it when jazz hands were a legitimate part of the first routine. But the two of us powered through it and were better off for it, even if that meant we would just have this shared memory.

"That was the most embarrassing thing I've ever done," Katie said shaking her head back and forth. She pointed an accusing finger at me. "Don't you dare tell anyone."

"I guess that means you don't want me to post the video I took online?"

She shot me a crude gesture with her hand before sitting down on the couch. "I would kill you if you took video of that mess."

"No video, but I'm still glad we did it." I sat down beside her with a smile still on my face.

"Gwen, are you okay? I mean, I know you usually have class right now, and you seemed upset when you called," Katie asked turning serious. It was the second time she'd mentioned it since being over.

I would have been happy to gloss over it. I didn't want to talk about it. Just having my best friend's company and doing that ridiculous video was enough for me. I should have known she wouldn't drop it easily.

"It's been a long week," I explained.

"It's only Wednesday."

She was right, which meant I still have had a busy couple of days ahead of me. Some potentially awkward as hell days coming up. "TV and ice cream?" I suggested instead of talking about it.

"Is it even a question?" she said getting up and going to the kitchen. We had gone through the motions enough times that we were a well-oiled, veg-out machine. I would get the TV going while she went to grab the junk food.

She came back out barely a minute later carrying the tub of rocky road and two spoons. "It's not too weird to eat this when it's so cold?" I shot her a look at the blasphemy. It never was too cold for ice cream. "You're right. What was I thinking?"

It didn't take long before we were cuddled up on the couch under a blanket shamelessly eating ice cream and fawning over David Tennant. The man had beautiful hair, what could I say? And what did it say about me that I obviously had a thing for boys who spent so much time styling their hair?

Ugh, I did not want to think about Mitch right now.

"How long do you think it takes for him to get it to stand up like that?" Katie asked while the intro played for another episode of our favorite show.

"I don't know, but could you imagine putting that on your resume? Yes, my skills include defying gravity and not passing out in the presence of the greatest time lord that ever lived."

"I thought you liked Tom Baker?" The actor who played the main character in the seventies.

"Can I tell you a secret?" I asked leaning in. Katie nodded. "I just have a thing for his scarf," I whispered like I was sharing some great secret. That would be a great project to attempt now that I'd successfully finished my beanie.

My friend shook her head. "You seriously are the best. Did you know that?"

"Because I like a scarf?"

"No, because you are your own person. You don't care what anyone thinks. I love you for it." She leaned over and gave me a hug along with a loud kiss on the cheek. Then propping herself back into position she settled her attention back on the screen.

I knew she didn't mean it as an insult, but I couldn't help but be offended by her words. Of course I cared what people thought about me. Didn't everyone? But for her to think that I didn't care at all made me wonder if I was really that weird.

My thoughts were going crazy. I hated that I was over-analyzing Katie's words the way I did. It was just another symptom of my overanxious lifestyle. That I couldn't stop thinking about whether or not she meant anything by them to the point that I didn't even realize we had finished yet another episode.

Katie stretched her arms above her head and yawned. "I love you, *chica*, but I promised Julian we would go do something later. I think it's time for me to head out."

"If that will get you to put your arms down, then get outta here," I teased, smacking her arms down. She didn't actually smell, but I wasn't going to tell her that.

"Oh, it's on," Katie said while trying to force her armpits in my face. What happened to my reserved friend who moved here this past summer? Not that I was upset or anything. I loved seeing her as she came out of her shell over the last few months. The more she opened up, the better our friendship had gotten.

"You are so gross," I yelled at her, wiggling out of her grip. "I don't think Julian's street cred is the only thing wearing off on you," I said as I finally got out of her reach.

"Are you saying Julian smells?"

"Only in the worst way." I smiled.

"Oh, I'm telling him you said that."

"Don't forget that I used to work with him. There were plenty of times I told him exactly how bad he smelled after spending a night in the hot kitchen."

"I used to work with him, too, but I will deny that he smells bad until the day I die," Katie said as she made one last attempt to shove my face in her armpit. "And if you ever tell anyone I did that video with you, I'll deny it."

"Your secret's safe with me," I said as she walked out the door. It was such a cliché thing to say, and the words hit too close to home. Of course, Katie could always trust me with her secrets. I just wondered when I would extend the same courtesy to her.

CHAPTER FOUR

MITCH

I WAS STILL HURTING from Gwen's very blatant rejection. I was somewhat used to it, but this was the most painful incident yet. When she texted me the next morning saying she was driving herself to school the next day, I knew that she was just as affected by it as I was.

Whether that was good or bad was to be determined.

I had considered not going to The Farmhouse, but I found that it didn't matter what had happened. I didn't want to stay away. The food at the diner was good, they had amazing burgers, but the real reason I went was to see Gwen. It was a standing appointment every week. On Thursday nights, I came and ate in her section.

I wasn't going to miss it just because I tried, and failed, to kiss her. A little awkwardness could never keep me away.

As I walked into the diner, I peeked over the hostess podium that stood at the entrance. I never really understood why it was there. The restaurant was a hole in the wall that only had a handful of employees. A hostess wasn't on the payroll, but I knew the podium had a chart on it showing which waitress had which tables. It looked like

Gwen was working with Sarah that evening. Sarah had one end of the dining room, Gwen had the other. After figuring out what side was hers, I walked over to a booth and sat down.

The place was a River Valley staple. Having grown up in this small town, I couldn't remember a time when I hadn't come here. Milkshakes after t-ball when I was a kid. Burgers after football games when I was in high school. Everyone ate here. No exceptions.

IT WAS SNOWING outside when I got there, and I had dressed in warm clothing. Once inside, the heat of the building hit me. I had a feeling Gwen had been in charge of the thermostat for the evening. Between the heat coming from the vents and the heat that surely would be coming from the kitchen, I found myself burning up in no time.

My jacket, hat, and gloves were off quicker than I could say heatstroke.

"Damn, Gwen," I said when she made it over to the table with a soda. "Mike must not be here tonight. He would never let you get away with this."

Mike was the owner of The Farmhouse. If Gwen and Katie were to be believed, he was the biggest tightwad that ever lived. He'd probably set the thermostat to the same temperature as the air outside.

"Why would you assume this was my doing?" she asked aghast, but I could see the guilt in her eyes.

"You're as bad as Katie."

"I used to live in Cali. Surely I have an excuse?"

"You've been here for a few years, though. I'd think your blood would have thickened by now."

"I think I could spend a thousand years in River Valley

and I still wouldn't acclimate to the winters here." She laughed. "And, yes, the heater was my idea. Is it that bad?"

I looked around at the other people in the restaurant. No one looked uncomfortable, but I couldn't resist. "I mean, that guy looks like he's about to melt." I tipped my head in the direction of a nearby booth. "And I'm about to start a strip tease if it doesn't cool down soon."

"Looks like you already started," she said pointing to the pile of discarded clothing next to me.

"Just wait and see."

"It's not even that bad. I only set it to eighty."

"Eighty!" It was warm inside, but the temperature still surprised me. "Are you serious Gwen? Turn it down and then come back and hang out with me."

"Fine. I'll be back in a couple of minutes, but I'm not going any lower than seventy-five," she said defensively like I was going to start arguing.

I just grinned as she walked off.

During our short conversation, neither one of us addressed what happened the other day. I wondered if we were going to pretend like it never happened. Sometimes we talked about the awkwardness between us, but most of the time we ignored it. I wanted to talk this time. I wanted us to get everything on the table, but I would let Gwen be the one to initiate.

What would it look like to openly discuss our feelings? I tried to imagine Gwen talking honestly about how she felt instead of covering everything in layers of innuendo and false ignorance. It would mean I would have to be serious. I wanted to be serious.

I wasn't left long with my thoughts before Gwen came back with a plate containing a burger and fries. I knew she placed the order before even greeting me with my drink. I always got a burger, and Gwen was so good about remembering that kind of thing. She was an excellent waitress. She always brushed me off when I told her, but I knew she genuinely cared that her tables were taken care of.

"Man, it's dead tonight," she complained while sitting down across from me. I started eating my food. "I'll be lucky to break double digits in tips."

"Maybe you could flirt with your tables," I suggested around a bite of my burger.

"You're my only table, Mitch." She sighed before noticing I was batting my eyes suggestively at her. I even went so far to prop my chin in my hand like a blushing debutante. "Oh, my goodness. You are the worst, did you know that?"

I sat back up. "Just for that, you're getting a penny turned face down on the table."

"Ugh. That table was the worst. They had me running all over the place that night."

"Don't forget the note they left with your *tip*."

"How could I forget?" She cleared her throat and began to speak in a nasally voice. "Miss, it gives me no pleasure to write this, but I do hope it will be a help to you in the future. When a drink is empty, your customers expect you to refill it. Let this penny be your reminder that good customer service always wins."

People could be real jerks sometimes.

She pulled out her keys and proudly displayed the penny hanging from it. She had drilled a hole in it and put it on a ring the next day. "I still haven't had the heart to spend it." Her hand lifted to her eye as she pretended to wipe a sentimental tear from it.

"Wouldn't want to blow it all in one place."

"I'm saving it for retirement," she said and put her keys back in her pocket.

There wasn't much to say after that, so we sat in silence while I continued eating. It wasn't exactly awkward, but it wasn't companionable either. Gwen looked lost in her thoughts, and I could easily let mine wander as well. I didn't want that. I came in to see her. I racked my brain for something witty to say.

It was nearly impossible not to ask about the other night. The more I forced myself to think of something else, the more my mind wanted to cry out. I was afraid my mouth was going to say something in some weird word vomit, so I blurted out the only other thing I could think of.

"Let's say you could have any superpower in the world, what would it be?"

If she was surprised, she didn't show it. "Right now?"

"Sure."

"Atmokinesis."

Leave it to Gwen to avoid picking something easy like flying or mind reading. "Is that even a real power?"

"Of course it's real. It's the power to control the weather," she said waving her hand at the window. "Right now, I'd make it stop snowing."

"Of course you would." Gwen was a Cali girl, through and through.

"What about you? What would you choose?"

"Invisibility," I answered matter-of-factly.

At this, she let out a huge laugh. Not the pity laughs we usually gave each other, the kind that came out when a friend said something amusing but not deserving of genuine laughter. This was genuine. "You are so full of it. You wouldn't choose invisibility if your life depended on it."

I couldn't help but laugh with her. "Yeah, you're right. But I don't have the catalog of superpowers memorized like you do. Invisibility just sounded like the right answer." I shrugged.

Gwen leaned in over the table between us. "Right now, you'd probably wish you have superhuman senses."

"Oh, yeah? Why is that?"

"Because then you'd be able to detect the spit in your drink."

"Is it yours?"

"Obviously." She raised her brows and crossed her arms across her chest, doing her best to give me a haughty stare. It was so darn adorable. I knew she would never spit in someone's drink, even if they deserved it. Plus, there was the fact that I didn't deserve it.

I took the straw out of my drink and lifted the glass to my lips drinking every last bit of soda, never letting my eyes leave hers. "That was the best drink I've ever tasted." I winked at her.

"You are so gross."

"I've done worse. Does eat off mean anything to you?" I asked remembering a particularly disgusting memory. I literally ate food that had come out of her mouth. Not my proudest moment, but you do what you gotta do to win.

"You got me there." She let out another genuine laugh. It was one of the best sounds in the world. "I didn't spit in your drink."

"I know."

"Maybe I will one day."

"I highly doubt that. There's not a mean bone in that body of yours."

"Whatever. So what superpower would you really choose? Invisibility doesn't count."

"You didn't give me a real answer either," I reminded her.

"Time travel," she said without hesitation this time. That would be cool. "Your turn."

"If I could fly, we could be a crime fighting duo. You could take us to some awful point in history, and I could swoop us in to get the bad guys."

"Gwen and Mitch, defenders of the innocent."

"I think you meant, Mitch and Gwen, vigilantes for hire."

She shook her head at me and opened her mouth to say something else, but the bell on the front door jingled. She gave me a lingering glance before she got up to greet the newcomers. "Wish me luck with these customers. I heard the guy at my other table was a total jerk."

"The worst is what I was told."

She gave me one last smile before walking away, and I finished what was left of my meal. I watched as another group walked in and knew I lost her for the night.

Gwen would occasionally come by my table to refill my drink or make sure I was okay, but she spent most of the time taking care of her legitimate tables. At one point, she brought me a piece of pie, on the house. I made sure I left a penny face down on her table before I left, but made up for it by putting a bigger tip on my credit card.

I enjoyed our Thursday night dates, if that's what you wanted to call this. I wanted to think it would lead to something else eventually. But with recent events, I feared I might be firmly in the friend zone.

I left contemplating how much longer I planned to do this.

CHAPTER FIVE

GWEN

IT SEEMED like it had been forever since I'd seen Katie. It wasn't the case, of course. I'd just seen her a couple of days ago. But things were so different from when we first met. In some ways, it was better. We were much more comfortable around each other now. In other ways, it was worse. I felt like I barely saw her. She was dating Julian, and they were still in the honeymoon stage.

Calling it a honeymoon was an understatement. The two were joined at the hip. It reminded me of this skit I saw on TV once about a toilet made for two. Basically, it had two seats, so more than one person could use it at the same time. I laughed out loud at the idea of them going to the bathroom together as I walked up to my friend.

"What's so funny?" Katie asked tying her apron around her waist. We were working lunch shift together, something that rarely happened these days.

"Oh, this cat video I watched before coming in," I lied not wanting to admit where my mind sometimes went when I got lost in my thoughts. *Oh, you know, I just wondered if you and Julian might ever poop with each other since you can't seem to be apart.*

"Huh," she said skeptically studying my face. "Must have been pretty funny."

I didn't answer, but instead started getting some of my things together for the lunch rush. I made sure I had a pile of small bills for change and my coveted purple pen. I'm not sure what it was about pens and restaurants, but they were always going missing. My favorite one stayed tucked in my apron so it couldn't grow legs and walk off. I knew it was silly, but there were small pleasures to be found when I worked. A pen that glided across the paper tickets was one of them.

I looked over to see Katie going through the same mental checklist, getting ready for our shift. Fridays were always busy during lunch. We had the white collar guys who were over brown bagging it or local college students who didn't have class. You never knew who would come in, in an attempt to start the weekend early.

"How's Julian?" I asked Katie as we sat down at one of the booths waiting for the diner to open. I had a drink and a small salad I was trying to get down before people showed up. We still had a few minutes of peace before everything went crazy, and I was curious how my long-lost friend was doing. Between Julian getting fired from the diner and life's general business, I never saw him anymore.

Katie's entire face transformed at the mention of his name. I swore if she smiled any bigger, her lips were going to crack. Her skin started glowing. How was that even possible? "He's good."

"Any luck on the job front?"

"Not yet. But Gwen, I am so proud of him. He has been

busting his butt this semester with school. Before you know it, we'll both be at BSU with you and Mitch."

I groaned at her words.

Katie always broke the four of us up into couples. Everything felt like a double date when both Katie and Mitch were involved. Katie always brought Julian, and they paired off essentially pairing Mitch and me together. I couldn't find neutral ground. If defining my relationship with Mitch had been difficult before, now it was impossible. I wanted to stay friends, while everyone else pushed for more.

"Katie, we're not dating. You know, you could be joining just me at school. Or just joining Mitch. Maybe you're joining Michelle and Mitch. Or, heaven forbid, Michelle and me. Or even Thomas."

"Who's Thomas?" Katie interrupted my rant.

"Just some dude in one of my classes." I waved my hand at her like I was swatting away an imaginary bug. "The point is, you two don't always have to be joining with the two of us because there is no us. It's me, and it's him."

Katie's brows rose at this. "For not considering yourself a couple, you certainly have given it a lot of thought."

"Maybe it's because we're lumped together so much."

"Or maybe the lady protests too much, methinks."

"Are you really quoting *Hamlet* right now?"

"Is it appropriate?" She leaned forward across the Formica countertop that separated us.

I sighed at the turn our conversation took. This always happened whenever Mitch came up. Katie found happiness in a relationship and thought that I needed to do the same.

Immediately.

"It's complicated, remember?"

"Yeah, that's what you keep saying. Listen, Gwen, I just

said you and Mitch because you guys both *happen* to be my friends and both *happen* to be at the same school Julian and I are planning on going to next year. I wasn't trying to start anything."

The bell on the front door saved me from having to respond to that. Katie had a point. I might have been protesting too much, just like Queen Gertrude. Hopefully, that didn't mean my life was a tragedy.

I looked over as a mom with her two young children walked in. They were wrapped up in the most adorable jackets and hats. They looked like puffy, shapeless blobs with angel faces in all their layers. "That's all you, mama," I told Katie as I stood up and walked to the kitchen, bringing my dirty dishes with me.

She mouthed, "You suck," in my direction before walking off to greet her new table. I knew she hated cleaning up after the families with children who sat at her tables. There were always bound to be crumbs everywhere, and the odds of one of them spilling their drink on the table were high. I had my reasons for not wanting to have a table with kids.

Almost immediately after our first customers came in, a young couple walked into the diner. It meant I didn't get to hide in the kitchen for long. They were an odd couple for sure. The girl looked like a legit gypsy while her boyfriend looked almost like a rebel with his longish hair and leather jacket. Maybe opposites did attract, because they looked happy as they walked through the front door.

The girl, with her flowy top and bandana threaded through her blond locks, looked completely unaffected by the cold. She didn't wear a jacket over her clothing. The guy standing beside her looked like he would rather be anywhere that wasn't snowing. He wrapped his arms across the front of his chest to warm himself up.

While I wouldn't pretend to know everyone in River Valley, the town was small enough to know when someone wasn't a local. This couple was definitely from out of town.

"You guys aren't from around here, are you?" I asked after walking them to a booth in my section.

"What was the giveaway?" the boy responded, not looking at me, but instead giving the girl across the table from him a pointed look.

"I think I'd remember seeing you. I assume you're just passing through?"

"Yep. I'm Charlotte, but you can call me Char," she chirped before pointing to the boy sitting across from her. "And that's Chase. We're actually from Florida, but we're taking a year off to explore the country."

"Thus the RV out front," he chimed in.

I took the opportunity to look out the window. Sure enough, there was a huge RV sitting in the parking lot of the diner. "Sounds like fun."

Charlotte started up again. "We've spent the past few months exploring National Parks like Glacier, the Cascade Mountains, Yosemite, blah, blah, blah. We just finished a few weeks in Yellowstone, but Chase couldn't take the cold anymore, so we are heading back south to see what there is to see in Arizona."

Sign me up with Chase. I was entirely over the cold weather.

"Have you ever seen Zion or the Grand Canyon this time of year?" she asked.

"Um, no. I pretty much stay put."

The girl gave me a look I couldn't quite interpret when I said this, so I knew it wasn't the answer she was looking for.

I quickly changed the subject back to food. "What can I get you?"

"You're the expert," the girl said. She waved her hand in my direction causing the bangles on her arm jingling with the small movement. "What do you suggest?"

"Well, The Farmhouse has the best burgers in town."

"Then, we'll have two burgers." She smiled at me, not giving Chase a chance to get a word in.

"Sounds good," I said slowly giving him one last opportunity to correct the girl he was with. When he didn't, I walked back to the kitchen to give the cooks their order.

It might have been rude, but I couldn't stop myself from watching them as they sat and talked to one another. I didn't have any other tables yet, and I was playing the stalker. They fascinated me. Even from my brief interaction with them, it was evident that they loved each other, but also obvious that they drove each other nuts. The girl was quite obviously the dominant one. Although, it didn't seem to bother Chase. I pictured Mitch and me in their positions, driving all over creation, stopping in at random diners along the way.

Would Mitch tease me like that? No doubt.

Would I ever be brave enough to do it? Probably not.

The guy looked over a couple of times while they waited for their food, catching me staring at them. Every time, I would quickly avert my eyes and start doing something to look busy. I shuffled the salt and pepper at an empty table. I wiped down a table that was already clean. At one point, Katie caught me doing one of those unnecessary tasks and gave me a questioning look. How could I explain the pull I felt for the couple at table five?

When I brought their burgers to their table, I couldn't

help but ask, "So, what are you guys doing in River Valley, besides eating gourmet cuisine?"

Chase's lips curved into a small smile, while the girl jumped in again. "We were hoping you could suggest something."

"Char's all about experiencing the local flavor," he added. That much was clear.

I might not be willing to go on adventures, but that didn't mean I couldn't encourage others in theirs, right? "Well, there are these caves. They're an old lava tube under the ground. A lot of people like to go there and experience total darkness. Could be romantic?" I suggested with a wink

"Oh, no," Char said.

At the same time, Chase said, "No, no, no."

They were both shaking their heads frantically.

"We're not a couple," Char clarified laughing. "We've gotten that a lot over the last few months."

"Guess it's not super common for a brother and sister to travel cross country together," her brother added.

Now it all made sense, why I could see Mitch and myself in them. There were siblings. They loved each other —just not in a romantic way.

I stayed at the table a little longer, mostly talking about traveling. Unfortunately, the discovery that they were related deflated me more than I realized, and I went through our conversation like I was sleepwalking. Smiling and nodding when appropriate, not registering what was being said. As more customers came in, I was able to excuse myself politely. Suddenly, my fascination with my table turned into frustration.

If I was going to date anyone, it would be Mitch. And, it turned out that our relationship was more brother/sister in its dynamics than boyfriend/girlfriend. That realization hurt and frustrated me. But wasn't I the one pushing him away in the first place? Mitch wanted a relationship with me. I was the one holding us back. It was possible Mitch never saw the sibling dynamics in the first place.

I couldn't sort my feelings out but knew the real hold up came from a place of fear, a fear I wasn't quite ready to vocalize.

I was afraid. Afraid to know how great it would be because I knew that once I got a taste, I would never want to stop. A relationship with him would be perfect, at least initially. Things never stayed that way though, if Ethan was any indication. I knew Mitch wasn't like him. But then, how could I know for sure?

Thankfully, it did end up being a busy shift, which meant I had little time to focus on all of this. I didn't even notice when the travelers left, except for the generous tip and note urging me to be adventurous left on the table.

When things had finally slowed down, I found Katie. I remembered Mitch's invitation from earlier in the week. In the excitement of the week, I'd nearly forgotten. "Come to a party with me tonight."

"Um, okay?" She looked confused. Possibly because I'd blurted the request without any preamble. Or, maybe because parties were not my scene.

"Mitch invited me," I explained.

"Ok, great. I'll invite Julian."

I didn't even realize I was setting myself up. It looked like another double date was in my immediate future.

Awesome.

CHAPTER SIX

MITCH

"MITCH, promise me you'll watch out for her," my mother begged across the dining room table.

Family dinner was pretty much non-negotiable at our house. My mom had grown up eating meals in front of the television or feasting on cereal for dinner by herself. She said she didn't want the same for us. So unless there was a good excuse for missing, we were all expected to be at the table by six o'clock sharp.

All of us meant both of my parents, my younger sister and me. Sam was a junior in high school, which meant it made sense for her to follow my parents' rules. On the other hand, I was a freshman at Boise State. I had thought that when I finally became a college student, I would have more freedom. I was learning that only applied to college students who didn't still live at home.

Rules certainly didn't apply to my older brother, Luke. He had very wisely gone to school in California. He was living the dream doing whatever he wanted, whenever he wanted. If Gwen was to be believed, the weather in California was fantastic, too. There were times I wished I'd gone away for school. I'd love to experience total freedom.

Living at home wasn't all bad, though. No rent, hot meals every day, plus my mom still did my laundry. Things could be worse.

"Don't worry, Mom," I answered her around a bite of chicken. "Brett's parties are lame."

"You're lame," Sam shot back and rolled her eyes. The attitude caught me off guard. She wasn't usually moody.

"Um, anyway." I shot my sister a look before I turned my attention back to Mom. "Even Gwen is coming tonight. If nothing else, that should tell you something about the party."

"Oh, is she?" My mom clasped her hands together. She was always trying to push the two of us into a relationship after meeting her for the first time a couple of years ago. "I'm so glad."

"It's about time," Sam mumbled under her breath.

I looked over to see her arms crossed over her chest. We typically had a good relationship, and any other time she would have been grateful that I was helping to put our parents at ease about going out. They were so overprotective of Sam because she was the baby of the family and their only daughter. I couldn't understand why she was acting this way.

"What's that supposed to mean?"

"Just that everyone knows she never goes out and does normal things, like a normal person."

"What would you even know about being a normal person? You're what, sixteen?" I could feel my irritation growing with each word my sister said.

"You're eighteen and still live at home."

"Stop being such a–"

"Guys," my mom interjected before I said something I would regret. "You will not speak to each other this way if you want to go to the party tonight." She leveled each of us with a stare.

What was it about moms and the look? It didn't matter how old I got, or what I got caught doing. If my mom didn't like what was going on, she would get me with a stare that made me feel like I was five years old again.

My sister and I both mumbled our apologies at each other before beginning to eat again. I didn't like the way she had spoken about Gwen. Sam didn't know anything about her.

The rest of the dinner passed in near silence. My mom and dad talked a little about work, politics, the typical adult stuff that I just didn't care about.

Not that it wasn't important. I knew it was. I just never understood why people were in a hurry to become adults with a bunch of boring responsibility. Seeing the uniformity of my parents' days made me realize just how important it was to live every moment until then.

When everyone finished their meals, and my parents were satisfied with the amount of family time we had together, my sister and I were excused from the table. We lived in a two-story house, and both of our rooms were upstairs.

I followed Sam up and grabbed her hand before she could walk into her room. "What is going on with you?"

"Just stay outta my way tonight. Can you do that?"

"Whoa, why?" Her voice had become harsher than it was downstairs. It wasn't like her to want distance. We had different interests, but it never caused a problem in our relationship.

"Just leave me alone this one time."

"Samantha."

"I mean it. Just hang out with Gwen tonight. Okay?"

"Fine." I lifted my hands in surrender. "I'll stay out of your way, but I'm still your big brother. Let me know if you're in trouble."

"Oh, my goodness, Mitch. I don't need a constant guardian, as much as Mom thinks I do. I just need some space from the bearing down from this family. I know you don't get it. Just please." Her voice began to lose its irritation with each word she spoke.

I had never had to worry about being overprotected. If anything, I wondered if my parents forgot about me between my older brother and younger sister. It was the curse of the middle child. I tried to imagine the situation from her perspective. "You're right, Sam. I'll back off. You still wanna ride together?"

"Jake will pick me up," she replied before finally stepping into her room and shutting the door, making it clear that the conversation was over.

I went to my room across the hall. It was bigger than my sister's because I still technically shared it with Luke. He would be back for spring and summer break. But for now, the room was all mine. His side was impeccable, and not just because he was away. He was always super tidy, to the point of being a little OCD. The bed was made, his desk free from any junk. Even the one poster on his side of the room was perfectly placed. Some cheesy mountain scene with a quote saying life was about the journey.

My side was a war zone. Pictures and posters were taped haphazardly on the wall, and clothes littered the ground. The only way to know if they were clean or dirty was to sniff them. I looked under the bed to try to find my favorite hat and saw six, no seven, half empty soda bottles.

Not having any luck with the hat hunt, I sat down on my bed confused about what was going on with Samantha. She got like this sometimes. I wasn't a complete idiot when it came to women's cycles having grown up with two of them.

My phone buzzed, and I grabbed it out of my pocket. A message from Gwen lit up the screen. I half expected her to pretend she was sick or something, but was pleasantly surprised.

Gwen: What time is the party?
Me: 10. You're not backing out, are you?
Gwen: I don't think so?
Me: I hope you figure it out.
Gwen: Katie's coming.
Me: Does that mean Julian's coming too?

Julian had been the outcast for a while and didn't usually do parties or big groups of people. But ever since he and Katie had started dating, he'd been getting out more and more. I didn't mind if he came. In fact, I hoped that he did so Katie wouldn't be the third wheel. Or worse, that I wouldn't be the third wheel to Gwen and Katie.

Gwen: Yeah. Do you mind?
Me: Nope. I'll pick you up at 10.
Gwen: You said it started at 10.
Me: Exactly.

For always claiming popularity in California, Gwen could be clueless sometimes. You never showed up on time.

Especially, if you were in college and going to a high school party.

After reassuring my mom that I'd keep an eye on my sister, I left to pick everyone else up and head to the party. Gwen was first, she was always first. And Julian and Katie lived on the same street, so I got them in one fell swoop. My truck had an expanded cab that was perfect for fitting everyone. It was older, but it did the job.

Brett's family had a few acres on the other end of town. As we got closer, we could see the blaze of the bonfire all the way down the drive. A couple of inches of mostly undisturbed snow covered the ground.

It was a beautiful sight. Like something you'd see in a painting.

The ride had been pretty quiet. I still wasn't convinced that Katie and Julian didn't take advantage of the dark on the way over. They couldn't keep their hands and mouths off of each other these days. I wondered if they'd been making out in the back seat while Gwen and I sat in the front of my truck's cab. I wanted to be the one making out in my truck.

I pushed the thought out of my head as we got closer to the actual house and I parked near some cars I recognized. Everyone hopped out quickly. Who knew a bunch of high schoolers with a keg was so exciting?

"Ugh. Why would anyone think a bonfire is a good idea when it's below freezing?" Katie said as soon as she got outside.

We all thought it was cold, but she took layers to a new level. Over her scarf and beanie was a parka with a hood. I could only guess how many sweaters she had on underneath the thing.

Gwen wasn't much better. She had a heavy jacket,

scarf, and hat but was still shivering from the cold. It cracked me up.

"Boo-hoo, I miss sunshine and saltwater. I don't like being cold," I said with an exaggerated whine to my voice.

"You owe me for this," Gwen said before punching me in the arm. "Katie's right, it's freezing."

I looked over to Julian for some help, but the dude was already whipped. He just shrugged and shook his head indicating he wasn't getting involved.

"Fine. Let's get the beach babes to the fire so they can thaw out."

Julian and Katie walked off, but I didn't make a move to get closer despite my suggestion. Gwen and I stood near each other awkwardly. I was curious to know if she was thinking about our almost kiss. I hadn't been able to stop thinking about it.

"I hope you have fun tonight," I leaned over and said, but I could see she was uncomfortable. I couldn't explain how, but seeing her stand as stiffly as she was, I knew her thoughts weren't in the same place.

"I don't like parties," she said confirming my suspicions and forced a smile.

"I know," I said grabbing her hand and threading my fingers through hers. "But I promise it won't be as bad as you think."

She looked unconvinced, but accepted my hand without protest and walked over to the fire with me. A couple of guys were passing out red solo cups, presumably filled with beer from the keg. Gwen shook her head when she was offered one. I followed her lead and refused one too.

Honestly, I liked having a drink when I was out, but I didn't need alcohol to have a good time either. Life was fun enough sober if you were willing to enjoy it. Drinking a beer when it made Gwen so uneasy wouldn't make the night better.

We kept moving to where everyone was congregated around the large flames in hopes of warming up. Once we had been sitting next to the fire for a few minutes, I thought Gwen would start to relax. Instead, her body stayed rigid next to me, and her eyes kept darting all over the place. I could see Julian and Katie on the other side laughing together. They stood by a few picnic tables away from the crowds. The light coming from the fire made it easy to spot them though.

"Gwen, do you wanna go find Katie and hang out with her?"

She looked over at me, seemingly surprised that I was standing next to her, even though I hadn't left her side or let go of her hand the entire time. She blinked a few times before responding, "Yeah, I think that's a good idea. You don't mind?"

"Nah," I answered. I hadn't seen my sister since we had arrived and it was time for me to touch base with her anyway considering that was the entire reason I came. I pointed to where I saw her friends and watched as she walked away.

I wasn't surprised when I missed her almost immediately after she left.

CHAPTER SEVEN

GWEN

"PLEASE TELL me you're not drinking from the cup Brett just gave you," I cried at Katie when I walked up. Julian was standing next to her and averted his gaze quicker than I thought possible. He wasn't used to seeing this side of me. When we worked together at the dinner, he usually only saw the cheerful Gwen that I tried to show the world.

"Seriously, Gwen, what is going on with you tonight? It isn't you to spaz like this."

Apparently, Katie wasn't used to this side of me either, despite our growing friendship.

I could tell my anxiety was getting worse. It made me worse. The party didn't help, not figuring out what the hell was going on between Mitch and me didn't help. I could feel the pressure building each day and wasn't sure how to stop it. I barely recognized the girl I'd been transforming into the last few months. I closed my eyes and counted to ten before responding.

"Sorry, I just really hate parties," I mumbled knowing I sounded like a broken record.

The chances of someone trying to drug Katie right in front of Julian were slim, I knew that. Plus, if something happened, I trusted him to take care of her. Old habits died hard, I supposed.

"Come on." Katie looped her arm through mine. "Some guys are playing some cheesy songs around the bonfire. Let's go sing along."

I looked over at her aghast, I loved to sing, but never in front of big crowds. My voice was terrible, and she knew that.

Katie just laughed. "Fine, let's just go listen to how terrible everyone else is," she said before dragging me away.

"What about Julian?"

"He's a big boy. He can handle himself. Can't you, babe?" she asked him.

"Have fun," he said smiling at her. It was obvious the boy adored her. I was so happy to see some of my best friends find happiness with each other. "I guess I'll try to go find Mitch or something."

Katie blew a kiss at him before steering us toward the fire. "I was freezing standing over there," she admitted once we were out of earshot. "I just hope no one plays Dave Matthews."

"If they do, I promise to sing until they stop."

"Perfect." She smiled. "Gwen, really what is going on with you?"

"I'd rather not go into it right now."

"You don't seem like yourself tonight."

Man, I was tired of hearing that. "How exactly can I be anyone other than me? I'm sorry if you don't like this part of me."

"Gwen, I'm not picking a fight. I just hate seeing you so uncomfortable. That's all."

"I'm fine," I said shutting down our conversation.

Katie was smart enough not to push any further. And, thankfully, she loved me enough not to leave me either.

We sat together warming ourselves near the fire, listening to some guy play the same three chords on his guitar singing like It was a huge talent to do so. It was mostly decent songs, and a bunch of people were singing along. I regretted snapping at Katie. I knew I was acting like a bitch for no reason.

I looked over to see Katie relaxing to the music. When she smiled at me, I knew that she wouldn't hold this against me. I started to relax too. And, if I allowed myself to admit it, I realized it was possible to have fun at a party after all.

A few songs into it, Julian showed back up and wrapped his arms around Katie. I tried to focus on the fire and the other people sitting around it but found my gaze wanting to go to them. She leaned back into his arms and looked so comfortable. So safe. I was jealous of that feeling. I wanted that. And yet, I was terrified of letting Mitch in any more than he already was.

I watched as the object of my musings talked to the guy with the guitar as soon as he finished the latest song. What was he up to? With Mitch, you never knew. The boy was goofy and clever at the same time, always trying to find new ways to suck every last bit of adventure from life.

When guitar guy, I couldn't remember his name, started playing a new song, I instantly knew what Mitch had planned.

You had to be kidding me.

I gaped at Mitch in horror as he grabbed a large stick off the ground and held it in his hand like a microphone. He started doing a weird sway-dance move and jumped up on a log drawing everyone's attention to him before walking toward me. The song he requested was the cheesiest love song I'd ever heard. I was always complaining to Mitch about the lyrics and the unrealistic nature of it.

"I would dieeeeee without youuuuuuu," his voice rang out in the night. People who had just been talking stopped to stare. "You are my shiiiiiining star. No matter how faaaaaar."

I felt a blush cover my cheeks. It was a weird sensation to be shaking from the cold, but also to feel my body heating up at the same time.

He clutched his free hand to his chest as he belted out the high notes of the refrain. "I will always be there!"

With every line he sang, he got closer until he was directly before me. I glanced over to Katie and Julian. They were fighting back laughter.

When Mitch sunk to his knees in the snow in front of me, I heard, rather than saw, the laughter spilling forth from my *former* friends. Those traitors.

I was so embarrassed, I did the first thing that came to mind. I pushed Mitch. I pushed him hard enough that he fell back into the snow. There were a couple of gasps, the laughter from beside me abruptly stopped. Even the music stopped. I could feel everyone's eyes on us and regretted my reaction.

But none of this stopped Mitch.

He laid in the snow laughing for a few seconds before getting up and brushing the snow off his arms. He turned toward the guy with the guitar. "Yo, Cooper, why'd you stop?" He gave me one last look I couldn't decipher before starting right back up with the song he'd been singing.

He walked up to a bunch of younger girls who were obviously very nervous about being at a party like this. Probably freshman. He started serenading them like he hadn't just been pushed into the snow. As if nothing had happened at all. The girls giggled furiously, sometimes stealing looks at me, trying to see if I would react. Most likely trying to decide if we were dating or not.

That was the thing about Mitch, though. He never got embarrassed. And he never took life too seriously. If one girl shot him down, which isn't exactly what had happened, he would move on. If a path was blocked, he would find a new one.

It was also the reason I knew whatever was going on with us would never work. I needed someone who would stick by me when things got hard. Because let's face it, I could be difficult. I needed someone who was willing to take the path with more resistance. I had been burned by that before. I was never making that mistake again.

"What was up with that little display?" Julian asked when the song had finally finished.

"Are you really going to try to explain Mitch and Gwen's relationship?" Katie answered for me, not giving me a chance to explain.

"What do you mean?" he said turning toward Katie, shutting me out.

"Seriously? You've been friends with Gwen longer than I have. Please tell me you've noticed the weird tension between the two of them."

Julian shrugged. "You're not wrapped up in everyone else's drama when you're consumed with your own."

Katie stepped away from her boyfriend and crossed her arms. "Julian Alvarado, do not pretend that you haven't seen the bedroom eyes those two have been making at each other for the last several months."

They were arguing over my non-existent relationship

with Mitch like I wasn't standing right there listening to every word they had said.

"Hello? I'm still here. And for the record, there are absolutely no bedroom eyes happening between the two of us." I practically yelled the last few words.

"Who are you making bedroom eyes with?" a familiar voice said from behind me.

I whipped around to see Mitch smirking at me. He must have walked up while I was listening to my soon-to-be-dead friends talk about me.

"No one," I answered at the same time as Katie said, "You."

I wanted to growl in exasperation but settled for shooting her a look instead. I was promising pain with my eyes, shooting imaginary daggers.

She shrugged a single shoulder in response.

"I think I'd know if Gwen was giving me eyes. I'm sad to report, she's right. No seductive looks to be had." He slung his arm over my shoulder and squeezed while shaking his head.

Sad to report?

Said the guy who went and flirted with a bunch of freshmen as soon as I pushed him away. And who did he think he was leaning against me after embarrassing me?

I pushed him again. Hard.

He stumbled back but kept his footing this time. I expected him to freak out. Instead, I watched as a brief look of hurt crossed his face before he gave a subtle nod to Julian and Katie sending them away. He walked toward me.

"Gwen," he said slowly, his voice calm.

My mind cleared from the red I had been seeing only seconds ago, and I was instantly ashamed of the way I had been acting. Why was I doing this?

"Mitch, I'm sorry." I closed my eyes refusing to look at him.

I felt his arms wrap around me and pull me close to him. It was unbelievably cold out here, even with the fire and the layers I put on before coming. His body was warm, and I felt myself leaning into him. Whether it was for the heat he was giving off or the comfort he was trying to give.

"No. I'm sorry, Gwen. You told me you didn't want to come and I pushed you anyway. This isn't your scene." He stopped briefly before going on. "Listen, I still have to touch base with Sam really quick. But as soon as I do, we'll go. Okay?"

"But we haven't been here that long. Won't you be upset?" I argued weakly, even though I wanted to go.

"Gwen, it's a high school party. I'm fine. Besides, my reputation would be ruined if I didn't keep up appearances and act like I had other places to be."

I knew he was giving me an out. There wasn't much to do in River Valley. That meant parties, even high school ones, were one of the few ways to have fun around here. Knowing Mitch's desire to experience everything, I knew part of him wanted to stay. He was saying this because of me.

I squeezed him back. "Thank you."

"Gwen, you know I'd do anything for you," he said, his voice sincere. The dark timbre of it caused his chest to vibrate against my own.

It made me uncomfortable. The same feelings from just days ago threatened to resurface. I considered lifting my face and letting it finally happen. A small voice in the back of my head screamed the opposite.

I had to do something.

I leaned back just enough to look into his eyes. "Yes, but

would you dieeeeee for meeeee?" I sang completely out of tune, killing the moment we were having.

Mitch shook his head and laughed. "Give me a minute, and we'll go," he said before walking off.

I walked the opposite way to find Julian and Katie.

CHAPTER EIGHT

MITCH

I KNEW I shouldn't have gone over to the giggling girls after Gwen pushed me in the snow, but *she pushed me in the snow*. My pride had stung after her reaction, and not for the first time. I had just acted in the moment of frustration and continued like I didn't care. The thing was, I did care. If Gwen's reaction was any indication, she was feeling the tension between us as well.

Right now, I just needed to find Samantha and make sure she was okay. That way, when I got home earlier than I originally planned, I could answer my parents honestly when they asked if I kept an eye on her.

Yes, I saw Samantha at the party.

Yes, she was okay.

Yes, it was okay that I left before she did.

I felt sorry for my sister. I always thought that the baby of the family could get away with murder, that's what all those psycho-babble books said. Firstborns were the responsible ones, always reliable. That described Luke down to every single molecule in his body. Middle children were social but could be rebellious. That sounded about right.

And the baby was supposed to self-centered and manipulative. That wasn't Sam at all, but my parents didn't get the memo.

Poor Sammy. She was the only girl in our family besides Mom. This made her the target of my parents' attention. All of their attention was focused on their baby girl. Sometimes, I wondered if they remembered I was there at all. Don't get me wrong, I liked the space I was given, but everything seemed so lopsided in our family. Sam was feeling that way too if her earlier mood was any indication.

I finally found her near Brett's parents' house talking with her boyfriend, Jake. There weren't many people around the actual house considering the bonfire was set away from the building. People tended to congregate near the warmth. I could see a patio set on the back porch and they were sitting together at it. They hadn't been together long, but I liked the guy. He seemed to make my sister happy. As long as he kept that up, I was a happy guy.

It turned out, I wasn't going to stay happy.

As I got closer, I could see something was off. The first thing that struck me as odd was the fact that Sam was crying. Her nose was red, but not from the cold. I could tell, even several feet away from her, that her eyes were red and puffy. I knew my sister, and I knew that look.

The second thing I noticed was Jake's expression. He wasn't crying. In fact, he didn't even look upset. He sat there with a mask of indifference on his face and his arms crossed over his chest leaning back in his chair completely unaffected by the emotions coming from my sister. Was he breaking up with her? Did her hurt her?

I was not a violent person. Gwen would often tell me that I was friendly to a fault. Right now, all I could think about was kicking this dude's ass for hurting my sister. The scene before me brought out all my caveman instincts. For once, my parents and I were on the same page about protecting Sam.

"What the hell is going on over here?" my voice boomed across the clearing as I strode over to where the two of them were sitting.

My sister's eyes widened at the sound of my voice, taken aback by my anger, before putting her hands over her face. "Could this night get any worse?" she cried.

"Did he hurt you?" I asked, but didn't let her answer before turning to Jake and asking him, "Did you hurt her?" My voice was considerably more sinister with the second question.

He snickered and averted his gaze from me in a way that made me want to punch him on pure principle.

"Mitch, calm down." Sam stood up and grabbed my arm.

"Not a chance."

"Please, Mitch. Just relax," she urged.

"Yeah, Mitch. Relax," Jake said, his smile cruel. What was going on between them? "I'm outta here," he said before getting up and walking away as if he didn't have a care in the world.

I watched him leave through narrowed eyes before turning back toward my sibling. Her face was still puffy, even though the tears had stopped. She had green eyes, just like me, and her dark hair hung down to her waist. She was used to the weather and wore a thick jacket, but she still had her arms wrapped around herself.

This party was shaping up to be a real mess for everyone I cared about.

"Samantha, what happened? Did he break up with you?"

"I can't do this right now," she answered, shaking her head back and forth while a new wave of tears started streaming down her face.

I pulled her close and hugged her. "Sam, you're my sister. You can tell me anything. And if Jake deserves it, I'll go kick his ass."

"It's not like that."

"Then what is it?"

"I'm late."

"Late for what? If you need me to take you somewhere, just let me know."

"Mitch, I'm *late*," she said with much more emphasis, her eyes begged me to understand.

Late.

She didn't mean...

My sister was only sixteen. There was no way she and that bastard were having sex. Was she telling me she was pregnant? There was *no* way she was pregnant.

"Are you sure?" I asked, waiting for her to explain. Hoping she was confused about how the whole thing worked. "I mean, you can't be."

"I'm pretty sure I know my freaking cycle, Mitch. And, yeah, it turns out pregnancy is a very real possibility for me right now. That's why I wanted you to stay away from me tonight. I wanted a chance to talk to Jake about it and see what he had to say before my brother found out about it."

"You're right. I'm sorry." I ran my hands through my hair. This could not be happening. I did not want to see my sister's life ruined like this. I wanted to leave it at that, but I had to know. "What did he say?"

"I cannot believe we are even having this discussion right now." She lifted her hands to her face as if she covered herself it would all go away. "He said he doubted it was his, if I was even pregnant. He accused me of trying to trap him. He was awful."

"I'm going to murder him."

"You're not going to do anything. With any luck, he'll keep his mouth shut until I know what's going on."

"Mom is going to flip," I said still struggling to process everything.

"She doesn't need to know."

"Don't you think they have the right?"

Her eyes widened. "Mitch, you cannot tell Mom and Dad. Not yet. Promise me, you won't tell."

"Fine, I won't say anything. But, if you are...you know." I couldn't say the word. "You're going to have to tell them eventually."

"I know. Right now, I just want to go home though. Can I ride with you?"

"Of course. I was ready to head out anyway. Come on."

I wrapped my arm around my little sister's shoulder and walked back toward the fire. I hoped I could find Gwen and everyone quickly and get out of here. For the first time in my life, I was over partying.

I spotted my friends quickly and let them know we were leaving and that Sam was coming with us. Gwen instinctively knew that I wanted my sister close to me and went straight to the backseat with Julian and Katie. I knew riding in the back of cars gave her terrible motion sickness, but she did it without complaint. One more thing to like about her, but I didn't dwell on the thought. I was too focused on getting my sister as far away from Jake as possible.

I buckled in and started back toward everyone's houses. Maneuvering through the parked cars was more difficult than when we'd arrived because the crowd had continued to grow throughout the evening. With some patience, which I was short on, I finally got us out to the main drag. It was a little two-lane road with very little vegetation and old wooden telephone poles lining one side. Snow still covered the ground, but thankfully it wasn't snowing.

I didn't play the radio, and no one talked. The car was completely silent. I was grateful for the fact that I didn't drink tonight after all. If I had, I might not have been able to rush out of Brett's the way I did. I just wanted to focus on getting everyone home safely and then help Sam figure out what she was going to do next.

Unfortunately, it didn't matter that I was sober, or that I was focused on the road. It didn't matter because while we were driving, I hit a patch of ice and lost control of my truck. It didn't matter that I had been cautious as we skidded toward the pole off the side of the road.

And it certainly didn't matter when I felt the impact, and everything went black.

CHAPTER NINE

GWEN

I HAD NEVER BEEN in a car accident before, not even a fender bender. The entire thing was over before I even realized what was going on. When you watch movies or shows that have a collision, they always show the scene in slow motion while making the music or sound effects louder to build up the drama.

Out here in the middle of nowhere—with only one vehicle involved—it felt too quiet. One minute I was gazing out the window in an attempt to ease my weak stomach, the next I felt the impact. No one seemed prepared for what had just happened. It felt almost fake in its stillness.

That is, until everyone shook off the initial shock and started reacting. I could hear Katie freaking out beside Julian and he was repeating comforting words to her. His hands were gently patting her body to look for injuries. When he'd determined she was okay, he pulled her in for a hug.

I looked around me. Air bags had deployed, and it seemed like everyone was still in the truck at least. Thank goodness for seat belts.

"Mitch?" I leaned forward and put my hand on his shoulder. He didn't answer right away, his head leaned forward. I prayed he wasn't seriously injured. "Mitch," I repeated louder and shook with more force.

His head wobbled slightly as he regained consciousness. His movements were sluggish.

Holy crap, this was not good.

"Julian, call 911. I think Mitch is hurt." My eyes were focused on him as he became more aware of his surroundings. Blood dripped from a cut on his face, but when he turned his face toward me, his eyes were clear. I let out a sigh of relief before remembering Sam was with us.

My gaze shot to the passenger seat. Thankfully, she was also conscious and looked aware of her surroundings. She had substantially more cuts on her face, but face injuries always looked bad. I hoped it was a case of her looking worse than she was.

I heard Julian's voice as he talked on the phone with the dispatcher. He was doing his best to give them our location, even though we were on an empty desert road. Katie had her phone pressed to her face. "Dad?" she cried into the receiver. It looked like she was on the verge of losing it.

There was no way I was calling my parents. Instead, I opened the back door of the truck cab and stepped out into the cold night air. At least, I assumed it was cold. I must have still been in shock because I didn't feel it.

Trying to make myself useful and not knowing where to start, I walked up to Sam's door and opened it. Her eyes were wild as she looked down at where her hands were resting against her flat stomach. She moved them quickly when she looked back up and saw that I was staring intently at them. I knew that protective posture, that look in her eyes.

"Does Mitch know?" I whispered as quietly as I could while taking care to make sure my face was hidden from his view, just in case he didn't.

Sam nodded her head.

"How far are you?" I asked, still taking care to keep my voice quiet, not wanting to share the news with everyone in the vehicle. Mitch might know, but that didn't mean Julian and Katie needed to be included. From the way she looked at me, I doubted it was common knowledge.

"I don't know," she whispered. My face scrunched up in confusion, so she clarified. "I'm late. Oh, no. What if something happened?"

"Samantha, come here," I said reaching for her hand. She put her hand in mine and stepped out into the night air next to me.

I gave her a quick hug before looking her over. I checked her arms and legs, but I was also looking for visible signs that something happened to the baby. Would she be bleeding already if something did happen? I didn't know but felt a small measure of relief when I heard the sound of sirens getting closer.

"Listen to me, Sam. You need to go with the EMTs and go to the hospital. You look fine, but just to make sure. I'm sure the rest of us will be right behind you."

She looked completely shell shocked but nodded. "Don't call my parents, Gwen."

"I won't. But, Sam, you're still in high school. The doctors will probably call them."

"This can't be happening."

"You're going to be fine. Just calm down and let them take care of you. Worry about your parents later. Okay?"

"Yeah, okay," she said, her eyes filling with tears, just as the ambulance pulled up.

I ran over to the guys getting out, and I tried to fill them in on what had happened. "I think we're all okay. But, my friend, she might be pregnant. Can you check her first?"

They walked over to her and started asking a bunch of questions I couldn't hear. I took it as an opportunity to go back over to Katie and Julian who were standing outside of the truck now. Katie was shivering, but the both of them looked uninjured, like me. "Did you get a hold of your dad?"

"Yeah, he's on his way. Please tell me Mitch wasn't drinking," Katie demanded while looking over at him as he talked to a police officer. He must have pulled up while I was distracted with the EMTs.

"I don't think so. I hope not." That would be really bad considering he was underage and driving. This night kept getting worse and worse.

I watched the scene play out over the next several moments. Everything felt surreal. EMTs were focused on Sam and getting her ready to go to St. Luke's in the ambulance. The police were talking to Mitch about the accident. The fact that he wasn't being taken away made me believe he hadn't been drinking tonight. Thank goodness for small mercies.

At some point, Mr. Lynch, Katie's dad, showed up in his old Bronco. He ran to Katie and wrapped her in his arms before making sure she was okay. I listened to him ask her over and over again if she was hurt. For the second time tonight, I felt jealous of my friend who got so much comfort from those who loved her. First with Julian and now with her dad.

And, while I understood that Mitch was busy answering questions about what happened, I found I was disappointed not to have his reassurances. He was usually the one who would console me. I was the odd person out watching as things unfolded around me. I wanted someone to ask me how I was handling it. I hated that I couldn't call my parents, I hated that I felt so alone in this moment.

"You okay?" Julian asked walking up to me, an answer to my unspoken pleas. Katie and her dad continued to talk to each other just a few feet away.

"I think so. You?"

"Yeah. Even Mitch looks pretty good for what just happened. I just hope his sister is okay." He didn't know everything that was going on, but he had to be concerned seeing her getting loaded up in the ambulance.

We were both watching as they shut the doors with Samantha inside. Mitch ran over to the ambulance and started talking to one of the guys walking back to the driver's door. The quiet conversation soon turned into a loud argument.

"What do you mean I can't come? I'm her brother," he demanded.

"I'm sorry son. It's a liability. You can come up and see her as soon as you're done here," the older man said before hopping back into the driver's seat and heading off.

It looked like he wanted to argue further, that he might jump in the back anyway. Instead, his whole body deflated as he stood watching them drive away.

Mitch didn't stay that way. Once the ambulance was out of sight, he let out a string of curses that sounded wrong coming from his mouth and kicked his truck. Repeatedly. I gave him his space until he got most of his frustration out. I was not getting between him and his truck right now. What he must have been feeling, helpless to do anything for his sister.

I walked up to Katie and her dad, noting that Julian had

rejoined them while I was watching the scene with Mitch, just in time to hear Mr. Lynch say, "There's still a lot that needs to happen here. Mitch is gonna need to get his truck taken care of, and I'd still like to make sure you kids are alright. Maybe I can drive you all up to the hospital after calling a tow truck."

"Are you sure?" Katie said, sounding surprised.

"Katie-bug, I'm your dad. Of course I want to make sure you're okay. I'm happy to help your friends. I just hope you realize I'm also going to have to make sure I get in touch with everyone else's parents, too."

I groaned at his words. He was right but damn it. I was terrified to talk to my parents about tonight, even knowing I would have to. Mitch hadn't been reckless, but they would find a way to blame it on him. Or on me. They might even place the blame on Julian and Katie. Who knew?

The next hour was a blur as we went to the hospital and as Mr. Lynch called everyone's parents. What good was it to be legally considered an adult when you still lived at home and under their control? Everyone was all right, but that didn't stop the swarm of adults from descending upon us.

Julian's mom came and checked on him. Mitch's parents rushed through the emergency waiting room and were taken up to see their daughter. Katie's dad hadn't left his post across the waiting room. He was giving us space, but that didn't mean he was leaving. I wished my parents could show their concern without getting angry. I knew that would never be the case. Especially since our move to Idaho.

When my parents finally arrived looking completely disheveled, I felt like I was going to throw up. My nerves had been slowly getting worse as I waited for it. I held my breath waiting for them to start in on me.

"Gwendolyn Marie," my mother exclaimed when she got closer.

"Hey, Mom."

"Don't you *hey, Mom* me. I've been worried sick the entire drive over here. You promised me that you were going to make better decisions when we moved here. I cannot watch you destroy your life again."

"Mom," I cried squeezing both of my hands into fists to keep from losing my temper more than I already had. I looked over to see if Katie or Julian were listening to her words. Both looked as if they were struggling not to listen. It was hard not to though. The waiting room was almost empty except for us. "It was an accident. They call it that because no one *intends* for it to happen. This has nothing to do with–"

"You may not speak to me that way," my mother interrupted while my dad stood watching the exchange between us in silence. He could be just as strict as my mom, but he also chose when to pick his battles. Apparently, midnight car accidents were under Mom's jurisdiction. "We're going home. We can talk more about it once we get to the car."

"Mom, we haven't heard back about Sam yet."

"I'm sure one of your *friends*," she said the word with disdain, "would be happy to keep you informed. For now, we're leaving."

I looked back hopelessly at Katie and Julian. Mitch had sent one text giving us an update but had mostly been silent. They were still running some tests to make sure everything was okay. I was concerned about whether or not the baby was okay.

"I'll text you as soon as we know," Katie reassured me. "I'm sure it's fine since her family is with her, though."

"You're probably right," I answered. I had to trust that

Mitch would let me know more when he was able. I gave her one last look as I followed behind my parents leaving the hospital.

My parents were completely silent the entire drive home. I think that was worse than them yelling. It gave me plenty to worry about. What were they thinking? What would they say when they finally started talking to me about what happened? I picked furiously at the jacket I wore.

The thing was, I loved my parents. They weren't abusive or anything. I knew they loved me. They just had high expectations and were finding themselves always disappointed in me and my actions. Sometimes I thought they were right to be as overbearing as they were. My actions had caused them to uproot and move to Idaho.

My dad was an accountant, a job that could be done anywhere. That didn't mean packing up all our earthly possessions and moving to a small town was easy. I knew that even without the constant reminders from my mom.

When we finally got home, I got a lecture about picking my friends more wisely. "Gwen, you are eighteen years old and in college. I'm sure you think that you are the ruler of your life, but I feel like I should also remind you that you are still living at home. While you're under our roof, we expect better from you. If you don't think you can do that, you're welcome to move out."

"Mom, it was an accident. Mitch hit a patch of ice," I argued.

"Always defending those around you, Gwen. I'm sure Mitch is perfect, just like Ethan was perfect," my mother said knowing how hurtful the words were.

"That's not fair," I whispered.

"Honey, don't you know by now? Life isn't fair. Go get

some rest and think about the choices you want to make for your life," she said ending the conversation.

I wanted to argue further, to tell her that Mitch wasn't Ethan. But Ethan hadn't exactly been who I thought he was, either, and that was my biggest hold up in dating Mitch. That fear of not knowing who someone is. And that fear drove so much of what I did or didn't do. The fear of the potential consequences of not knowing what people were made of beneath the surface controlled my actions.

I knew that if I stayed and spoke what was really on my mind, my mom would get more upset. She would remind me of the many reasons we moved, as if I could forget. So I let her end the conversation with those words.

I went upstairs and thought about all that had happened tonight. I tried laying on my bed to meditate over what everyone said, the unspoken conversations told by body language. I analyzed Mitch and the song, the accident. Unfortunately, the more I tried to focus, the less I was able to. Soon, I found myself pacing my room. Shortly after that, I was walking to my closet.

Hidden away on the top shelf were a few keepsakes from my high school days in California. I kept them all in a small box.

I had lived in a small city near the border of Mexico. I thought about the warmer weather there and how it contrasted with the winter wonderland here. It would be so nice to wear shorts in the winter again. However, that was the only thing I missed about my hometown. Everything else could suck it.

For some reason, that didn't stop me from hiding away pictures and other odd and ends from my time spent there. In the box, there was a dried corsage from my first home-coming dance, a couple of concert tickets from shows in San

Diego, a hospital band from a brief stay when I was sixteen. And, underneath everything, was a picture of Ethan and me.

The boy who ruined me.

It was from some school function, although I couldn't remember what it was anymore. We had just started dating, and I couldn't believe that the star football player had picked me to be his girlfriend. Younger me beamed standing next to him. I had fallen hard at the time, seeing what I wanted to see. The cute boy at school who made the perfect boyfriend.

His blond hair was combed back, and he was smiling that stupid, crooked smile he always wore next to me. That smile used to make me melt. Now, I could see it for what it was. A practiced curve of his lips that he knew would bring girls running. I wondered how many times he gave that same smile to others, even while we were dating.

The hand he draped over my shoulder in the photograph used to make me feel safe, treasured. Now, even looking at this single picture, I could see the controlling nature of the arm he held onto me with.

I had been naïve to fall for the act. I didn't know better then, but I would never allow myself to make the same mistake again.

CHAPTER TEN

MITCH

THE MONITORS in the room kept beeping, and I couldn't think with all the noise.

My parents and the nurses kept reassuring me that everything was okay, that Sam was fine. I just couldn't comprehend why she was hooked up to so many machines if she was fine or why we hadn't been able to go home if nothing was wrong.

She was laying in the hospital bed in an ugly gown, the kind that probably opened in the back. Normally, I would crack a joke about her wearing something like that, but I couldn't find any humor in the situation.

There was an IV going into one of her arms and a blood pressure cuff on the other, going off at regular intervals. Between that and the nurses coming in every so often to check her vitals, I was feeling on edge.

Everyone kept repeating how lucky we were not to be hurt worse after our collision with the telephone pole. I guess most people didn't walk away from something like that as unscathed as we were. My parents gave all the credit to our guardian angels.

I wanted to argue, to tell her that angels didn't care about what happened to us. I knew there was another explanation. We hit the ice at the perfect speed and hit the pole at the perfect angle. It was that combination that made the accident so minor.

Not that it was minor. My truck was completely totaled, and I would have to get a new one. I knew I had lost consciousness for a short time, which was unsettling. Not to mention my sister was stuck in a hospital room.

I started pacing faster as I processed everything that happened tonight. Had it only been an hour or so since we left the party?

"Mitch," my sister said. "Seriously, I'm fine. Once they clear me, I'm jumping out of this bed and dancing." I stopped moving long enough to raise my brows at her. "Alright, maybe not dancing. But you heard the doctors, they said I appear to be good considering the accident."

I wondered—not for the first time—when the doctors said everything was fine, if that meant *everything*. That could be the only explanation for why she was still here when everyone else who'd been in the accident was free to go whenever they wanted.

"Hey, Mom, Dad, can I have a minute with Sam? Maybe you guys could go stretch your legs?" I said.

They both looked confused by my sudden push to get them out of the room, but after a shared look between to two of them, they relented. I didn't waste a second not knowing how long I'd have. I pulled a chair up to Sam's bed.

"Have they said anything about...you know?"

"The baby?"

I tensed up at the unnatural calm of her voice. "Yes, the baby. What else would I try to ask you about after getting Mom and Dad out of here."

"There isn't a baby."

I paused letting her words sink in, trying to digest them.

"Like, there never was? Or something happened? You can't be vague like that, not right now. Not after everything that happened tonight." My words tumbled out in a rush.

"There never was a baby. I asked the nurse when we first got here if she could find out for me and if she could keep in quiet. My fight with Jake was over nothing." Her voice was still eerily steady.

"If a guy can't accept the possibility of being a dad, maybe he should keep it in his pants."

"Mitch!"

"I'm serious. I saw the way he treated you after you told him. He's a jerk."

"He was just freaked out. I'm hoping once he realizes I'm not pregnant, we can talk about it."

No way, she was not defending that guy. He was an asshole. "What are you saying?" I asked giving her a chance to correct me.

"I'm saying, that I'm hoping we can work it out." She shrugged.

"You're in shock, thinking you were pregnant and getting into a car accident on the same night. There's no way you're thinking clearly. Or, maybe I need to get checked out because I'm mishearing you. Samantha, you need to break up with him."

"Mitch, you are not going to tell me how to live my life. Maybe that works with Gwen, I don't know."

"This isn't about Gwen."

"You're right. It's about me and *my* life!"

"And I'm not going to let you make a mistake!"

"Last time I checked, you were not my parent!"

I took a deep breath, forcing myself to calm down. She

was right. I wasn't her parent. I reminded myself how I'd felt earlier because of all the rules my parents had for her that never applied to Luke and me.

I was still pretty freaking pissed at Jake though. Even after taking a couple more deep breaths for good measure. Sam wasn't thinking through it clearly. "I know that. What if it happens again though?"

"We'll be careful."

"And if it happens anyway?"

"Stop getting all worked up over nothing. I'll figure it out if it ever comes to that. I don't need to stress out about a baby right now because I'm not pregnant."

"What?" my mom's voice rang out from behind me. We had been so deep in our conversation, neither one of us heard her come back into the room. Our parents couldn't have been gone more than a couple of minutes. Did they even walk around? Or did they just step outside the room and count to a hundred?

"That was quick," I said, ignoring the fact that our parents walked in at the worst possible moment.

"We ran into Sam's doctor in the hall. They're discharging her, and I wanted to come and tell you guys the good news," my mom answered, but her voice lacked enthusiasm. Her eyes didn't leave my sister. "Mitch, why don't you go give your friends an update and leave us a minute."

I looked back at my sister and saw the fury on her face. I mouthed, "I'm sorry," before walking out, but she just shook her head at me.

When I got to the waiting room, Katie and Julian were still waiting. They sat near each other with Katie's head resting on his shoulder looking up at the TV. It was playing late night news. I briefly wondered if our accident would be newsworthy. I hoped not considering there weren't any major injuries.

I looked around, but only saw a few other people scattered across the room. Mr. Lynch was sitting in one of the corners on the phone with someone, but he nodded his head at me in acknowledgment. There was an older couple off to the other side of the waiting room.

Gwen was nowhere to be seen.

"Her parents came and got her," Katie said when she saw me looking around. "She wanted to stay, but her parents were crazy and practically dragged her out of here."

I had met them a few times. They were strict, but I never saw them speak unkindly toward their daughter. "Really?"

"Yeah, it was weird."

"I guess I'd better text her and let her know that Sam is okay. You guys should probably go home too. They just told us they're discharging her anyway. Thanks for sticking around."

Katie surprised me by standing up and giving me a hug. We had known each other when we were children, and we had become friends over the last few months, but I wouldn't say we were particularly close. This was the first time she'd ever done more than playfully punch me in the arm. It didn't matter, I accepted it. It had been a long night, and I was close to my breaking point with everything that had happened in the last couple of hours.

"Try to sleep tonight and let us know what we can do to help."

"I will," I said as my two friends left with Katie's dad. I waited for my family to come out, wondering just how badly I messed up. The TV continued its cycle on the day's news and went on to the weather. I barely registered what the anchors were saying over my thoughts.

I pulled out my phone and texted Gwen.

Me: Just wanted to let you know that Sam's ok.
Gwen: That's great.

Dots lit up the screen as she typed on the other end and quickly disappeared. This happened a couple of times as I stared at my screen wondering what she could be typing. At least a minute or two passed before my phone buzzed again with a new message.

Gwen: Is the baby ok?
Me: Turns out she wasn't even pregnant.
Gwen: How is she doing?
Me: I said she was fine.

I couldn't figure out why she asked me something I had already given her an answer to. Another minute passed before Gwen sent one last text. It was the same as before with the text bubble appearing and disappearing before she sent it.

Gwen: Good night, Mitch.

I didn't answer for two reasons. First, I was tired and I wasn't sure why she was acting so weird. It might not seem possible, but I could tell she was being passive aggressive through a text. I pictured her rolling her eyes with her last message. She would deny it, but I knew better. That pissed me off. It was a hard night for me, and she wasn't making it any easier.

And secondly, my parents came out with Sam and were ready to go home. I shoved the phone in my pocket and followed them out of the hospital in silence. The drive home was quiet. I sat in the back seat of my parents' car with Sam. I wasn't sure what was going through her head as we sat there. I half expected her to give me the stink eye or maybe text me the things she wouldn't dare say in front of Mom and Dad.

Instead, she surprised me by resting her head on my shoulder. She didn't say anything, so I kept my mouth shut. I just let her rest against me until we got back home. Even when my back was stiff from trying to keep my shoulder steady for her, I didn't pull away or ask her to move. It was the least I could do.

It was past midnight when we finally pulled into the driveway. I knew I wasn't the only one who felt emotionally drained after the night. In fact, I'd bet that Sam was feeling more exhausted than anyone else. I walked behind her to our rooms as soon as we got inside. Each step was a struggle.

Sam stopped just before she walked into her room. I waited, holding my breath, waiting for the angry words I'd anticipated since we left. They never came. She gave me one last sad look before going inside and shutting the door.

I went to my room, too tired to take off my clothes from the night or even attempt to pull down the comforter that was haphazardly laying across my bed. My thoughts selfishly went to the girl who'd been plaguing me this past week before sleep overtook me.

I WOKE up the next morning to light shining in my

window. Having no dreams the night before, it didn't feel like I had slept. More like a long blink. A blink so long, all my surrounding changed while my eyes were closed. The sun was shining in through my window when I was sure it was still supposed to still be dark.

For a second, I wondered if the accident had been the dream, and that was why I couldn't remember anything, but the stiffness in my neck was all the evidence I needed that it had happened.

I ran into a telephone pole last night.

My sister ended up in the hospital because of me.

I could have hurt or killed my friends.

I got up and dressed enough to go downstairs and greet my family. I could hear the clanking of silverware and murmur of voices and knew that breakfast had started without me. I strained to hear what they were saying as I got closer. Everything was softer, more subdued than usual, but the chatter was still there.

Eating around the breakfast table on Saturday mornings was another one of my mom's requirements. Assuming we weren't staying at a friend's, my mom liked to make pancakes on the weekends and have us sit at the dining room table together. Apparently not even a traumatic event like last night's deterred her.

I sat down feeling uneasy but started fixing a plate. My family was carrying on like nothing happened. As if I didn't endanger mine and my friends' lives last night. As if I didn't drop a bombshell about Sam's activities with Jake. I didn't like it.

"Mitch," my dad said, setting his silverware down and looking toward me. "Mr. Lynch made sure your truck was towed last night. Make sure you thank him for that before you go figure out what needs to be done."

"Of course, Dad," I answered moving some food around on my plate, still not taking a bite.

My mom asked me to pass the syrup.

Sam told my mom how good the pancakes were.

Dad said something about his plans for the day before beginning to read the paper.

"Isn't anyone going to mention what happened last night?" I blurted, unable to take any more normal.

My dad let out a noise that sounded like shock. How was he shocked?

"You know, me driving straight into a telephone pole."

My mom spoke this time. "Mitch, we are just so glad you and your sister are okay."

"You're supposed to be upset!"

"Accidents happen."

"So, we aren't going to talk about it then? We're going to act like it was just another night?"

"Of course it wasn't just another night. But–"

"Can we please just talk about it?" My voice broke as I pleaded with my parents to address what happened. I wanted my parents to be shaken up, to show that they were as freaked out by everything that happened as I was.

"There's not anything to talk about. We have to wait on the insurance company before we can get you a new vehicle, but–"

"What about Sam?" I interrupted again and immediately regretted the words. I didn't want to drag her into this any more than I already had. I just wanted to get my parents' attention.

"Mitch," my mother cried as Sam pushed her chair back, stood up, and stormed away from the table.

"What's going on between Sam and us is none of your business. You shouldn't have brought it up." My dad set the newspaper back down and looked at me. "Do you want me to be upset you got into an accident? Of course, I'm upset it happened. The police report said you hit a patch of ice though and it wasn't your fault."

That's not what I wanted. I knew it wasn't my fault, but the lack of emotion coming from either one of them made me question whether or not they even cared. I wanted someone to fuss over me and tell me how happy they were that I was okay. Instead, I got texts from Gwen asking about my sister. I got pancakes from my mom and a talk about insurance from my dad.

Where was the concern? The outrage?

I ran up the stairs after my sister, my food uneaten. Sam's door was closed, and I knocked hoping she would talk to me. An angry, "Go away," was the only response I received.

I waited for a couple of minutes standing outside. I said I was sorry. I told her how I didn't mean to say what I did. I never heard another sound from the other side and eventually gave up.

I went to my room not sure what to do. Unless someone picked me up, I was stuck in my crazy house with my crazy family that was far too subdued considering everything. Not for the first time this morning, I wondered if they were all taking happy pills without me.

Me: Can you come get me. I seemed to have misplaced my truck.
Me: I'll buy you coffee...?
Gwen: Already on my way. See you in 5.

CHAPTER ELEVEN

GWEN

AFTER HIS JOKE about losing his truck, I thought Mitch might be playful this morning. That was the way he tackled difficult things that came into his life. He never took them seriously in the first place. But after driving out to Beans & Things while Mitch sat uncharacteristically silent next to me, I wondered if he was okay. He was lost in thought and acting weird, even for him.

The fidgeting I was so accustomed to seeing was missing. No fingers were tapping, no knee bouncing. He was like a living statue in my passenger seat. I didn't like seeing him like this. I prepared myself to be the listening ear he would need right now. So much had changed in the last 24 hours—less than that, really.

We sat at our usual table off to the side of the seating area. It was next to a window that faced an empty field. It wasn't snowing today and most of last night's covering was melting from the sun. Both of our drinks sat untouched on the table.

"Mitch, talk to me."

He looked up at me. "I'm waiting for you to tell me I told you so."

"Are you serious?" Did he think I was so heartless? "I'm not happy something happened last night."

"You're always telling me how I need to be more careful."

"Only because I care about you."

"I would think that this would be the perfect opportunity to shove my face in it."

"You're my best friend, I don't want to be right."

"But you admit you think you were?"

"I'm not saying anything," I said a bit more defensively than I meant to.

He didn't respond, and I didn't add anything else.

This conversation was going all wrong. We were both stressed about the night before, and Mitch was looking to pick a fight no matter what I said. That much was obvious.

Mitch's drink must have been the most fascinating thing he'd ever seen because his stare didn't leave it for a second. His lips pressed together, the dimples I loved so much disappeared and reappeared as he worked his jaw. He was not going to speak first. I would need to be the one to extend the proverbial olive branch.

"I'm happy you're okay, Mitch."

This was the right thing to say, because his eyes lifted to mine, all irritation gone. "Me too. I can't believe no one was hurt."

"I know."

"I'm sorry I snapped at you."

"I wasn't trying to argue."

"I know. It's just this morning I thought my family would sit down and talk about everything, but they're acting like nothing even happened. I don't understand how they're so unaffected." He ran his hands through his hair, and I wondered if it was truly messy this morning. "I'm freaking out."

"Maybe they're not ready to talk about it yet? Maybe your parents don't know what to say."

I thought of all the times I disappointed my parents and how they could react in any number of ways. I never knew what to expect. I couldn't always figure it out, but they wanted what was best for me in the same way Mitch's parents did for him.

"Sometimes I wonder if they even care about me. Luke is off at UC San Diego, and Sam is the girl my mom always wanted. I'm just the kid who is stuck between them." He shrugged.

"How can you even think that?"

"You're, like, my best friend, which is the only reason I'm going to admit this. But I wish they would have been mad at me or something instead of putting all their energy into Sam."

"Maybe it was because she took an ambulance to the hospital?"

"It's because they found out she thought she was pregnant." When I gave him a questioning look, he added, "I accidentally said something in front of them."

"But she wasn't."

"We didn't know for sure for a while though." Mitch shook his head, not making eye contact with me, looking down at the drink in his hands. "What if she had been?" he asked, and in that question, I knew that was the other source of his irritability.

Mitch wanted his parents' to show concern for him, but he took responsibility for what happened to his sister too. The love he had for Sam was apparent.

"It would have been early enough that the baby would have been fine," I answered confidently after spending an hour researching accidents and pregnancy in the waiting room last night. I wanted to ease some of the tension he was carrying.

"No, I mean, what if she was pregnant? Her life would have been over."

He said it leaving no room to argue. To him, it was absolute fact. My heartbeat roared in my ears at his words. He didn't know—couldn't know. Unfortunately, it was the worst possible thing he could say to me.

I wanted to yell at him, pound my fists against his chest. I took a deep breath before responding, managing to keep it together. He was still shaken up and didn't realize what he was saying. I had to remember that.

"That wouldn't have been the worst thing that could have happened. I'm just thankful–"

"Of course it would have been the worst thing to happen to her," he interrupted. "Jake is a total waste of a human. What would she have done?"

"There are always options."

"Like an abortion? Gwen, you're talking about my sister."

"Actually, I meant adoption," I said impatiently, a fake smile plastered on my face.

"You mean give her baby up?"

I hated that phrase, that mentality. It was the same one I used to have. That was before.

I slapped my hands on the table. "First of all, Sam isn't pregnant. So, there isn't a baby to give up as you so crudely put it. The wording is important, Mitch. Second of all–"

"As if the way I say it makes a difference." Mitch shook

his head not letting me get to the rest of what I wanted to say. "I'm just glad she's not pregnant."

Before I registered what I was doing, I stood up and splashed my latte at him. The warm liquid hit him square in the chest. A part of me worried it would burn him. Instinctively, I started to move to clean him up. My lips parted to say I was sorry. I was always sorry. I fought against those things that had become so natural to me.

"As a matter of fact, the wording does make a difference to those women who choose adoption. I didn't give my baby up, Mitch. I placed her in a loving home with parents who would take better care of her than I was capable of doing."

His eyes widened in shock. Whether it was from the fact that I had just lost it completely or because I had just admitted my biggest secret to him in the middle of a coffee shop, I wasn't sure.

I didn't care that I was making a scene. I didn't care I was crying either, because it felt so good to finally tell someone.

I just wished it was under different circumstances because I could tell by the way Mitch was looking at me, this information turned his world upside-down. His mouth opened and closed a couple of times. I waited for him to say something. Anything. When he didn't, I decided I'd had more than enough for the morning.

"Look, I know I drove you here and all, but I can't be near you right now. You're going to have to find a different ride home."

"Gwen, wait."

I'd been in the middle of a grand exit but stopped to hear what he had to say. Please let it be the right thing, I prayed, not knowing what he could say that could make this moment better. I closed my eyes, bracing myself for his words.

"How could you keep that from me?"

It was the *wrong* thing to say. I opened my eyes to see his expression was one filled with hurt. He wasn't the only one.

"Goodbye, Mitch. Please don't talk to me until you can wrap your head around this without blaming me for not telling you sooner."

He didn't call out to me again as I walked out the door. Part of me was embarrassed to leave my best friend stranded and soaking wet. I hated how I left a mess for Janelle, the owner of the coffee shop, to clean up. There was just no way I could be in the same room as him a moment longer.

I drove just far enough away from Beans & Things to be out of sight before I stopped and let myself cry over what had just happened. The tears came easily, and my sobs filled the inside of my car. Anytime I thought too much about Janet, I would cry. I knew it had been the right decision, but I still struggled with missing my daughter.

My daughter.

Hearing one of my best friends talk so negatively about it made everything worse. I had always envisioned telling him one day, on my own terms. I imagined him encouraging me and reassuring me that it was a good decision. I would pull out the pictures I had of her, the ones I'd kept hidden in my secret box. He would smile at each one, his dimples deepening. He would tell me he didn't think less of me for what had happened. He would lean over and kiss me.

I punched my steering wheel several times.

Did I want any of that anymore? It was the dream. The reality was much more painful.

I grabbed my phone and texted Katie.

Me: I need to talk to you.
Katie: Oooookay. What's up?
Me: In person. ASAP.

My phone immediately started to vibrate with an incoming call. I shouldn't have been surprised when I saw her face light up my screen. After reassuring her I was fine but needed to talk, Katie calmed down and told me to come over. I was grateful to have a place to go. I wasn't ready to go home.

Katie lived with her dad, who was suspiciously absent when I arrived. He worked from home and was very much an introvert, so I knew she had something to do with it. A tub of ice cream and two spoons were sitting on the counter when I arrived. I started eating before greeting her.

"Kick your dad out?"

She smiled sheepishly for an instant but shrugged it off. "He needed to get out of the house anyway. You sounded pretty upset, so I wanted to make sure we had privacy."

"Yeah, it's not been a good day."

"Because of last night?"

"Because of Mitch."

Katie let out a long breath and smiled at me. "Gwen, I thought something was seriously wrong. Not that your fights with Mitch aren't difficult," she was quick to add. "But you sounded like the world was ending."

"I think my friendship with Mitch is over. It pretty much feels like that."

Katie looked at me confused. I wasn't making sense. This wasn't the way I planned to talk to Katie about my past either. We needed to have this discussion, even though it would be painful. I hoped she would be more understanding than Mitch had been.

"Katie, I told Mitch why we left California, and he didn't take it well."

At my words, she leaned forward. This was a discussion we had many times over the past several months of friendship. I had never been willing to reveal too much about my past, and she was always left curious.

I closed my eyes, afraid to look at her and started. "I was dating this guy in California, his name was Ethan. He was basically the most perfect guy you'd ever meet—great grades, never got in trouble, respectful to adults and kind to everyone at our school."

"Like Mitch," Katie said quietly, almost to herself.

"Like Mitch," I repeated. "We were dating for a while, and he brought me to this party. Just some stupid high school party. I had never been drunk before, hadn't cared about alcohol at all before that party. I felt so cool drinking all these mixed drinks with everyone. I thought I was so grown up. Ethan didn't even try to stop me when it was obvious I shouldn't have anymore."

I finally stole a glance at my friend sitting across the table. The spoon in her hand was forgotten, barely still being held by her fingers. Her eyes were wide, and I couldn't be sure that she was actually breathing. At that thought, I took a deep breath of my own and continued.

"He brought me upstairs and took my virginity."

Katie's free hand shot across the table and her fingers wrapped around my own.

"He didn't rape me, it wasn't like that," I quickly amended. "But it wasn't exactly how I imagined it happening, you know?" I let out a self-deprecating laugh.

"Gwen, I'm so sorry. That's awful."

I shook my head shaking off her words, willing the rest of the story to come "It's fine. There are worse things, right?

But a few weeks later, I started getting sick, and I realized I was pregnant."

Katie gasped.

"He dumped me before I could even finish telling him. So much for the perfect boyfriend."

We sat there for a few silent minutes. I wasn't sure what to say next.

"Janet," Katie guessed, breaking the silence. Her voice was gentle, not at all accusing.

I was thankful she made the connection. Months ago she saw a picture of my daughter and me tucked in the mirror on my dresser. The lie I had been encouraged to tell came out so easily. Janet was my "niece" in California. I hated being dishonest with Katie and was relieved to finally be talking about it with her.

I nodded confirming her suspicion. "Katie, it was awful. The lies Ethan told, the things people said. I went from being the girl everyone loved, to being tripped in the halls. But I knew this little girl deserved to have a chance."

"Gwen, you are one of the bravest people I know, to do that for your daughter."

I attempted to smile, but it was nearly impossible as I started crying. "My parents hated me for it. They tried to get me to have an abortion. I think they're still ashamed of me, disappointed in their little girl who ruined her life. I messed up so badly, we had to move to another state."

"You didn't mess up, Gwen. How could you even think that?"

I raised my eyebrows at her.

"Right, your parents. Well, from this day forward, I think you need to start thinking about it for yourself. Be proud of your decision." She was too cheerful, too optimistic.

"Yeah," I answered noncommittally. It was easy for her to say all that, not having lived with my parents for the last two years. She wasn't the one who had been reminded over and over of the *mistake* she made.

"What are her, um...what do you call the people who adopted her?"

I could see that Katie was trying. She didn't have any experience with this kind of thing. I gave her credit for wanting to know, for asking questions that were difficult for her.

"They're her parents, and they're wonderful. They love her so much. I get to go and visit her once a year. It was part of our adoption contract."

I pulled out my phone to show Katie the picture her parents texted from Janet's birthday. Most of the pictures I kept were hidden away, but I hadn't had a chance to save these particular images from my phone yet.

Katie smiled as I showed her the different scenes. Janet stuffing her face with a cupcake. Janet sitting on a swing at the playground. Janet smiling at the camera next to her adoptive parents.

"Is it weird?" Katie asked when I'd finished showing her.

"It's so hard, Katie." New tears streamed down my cheeks. "I can't even explain the pain I felt when I set her down for the last time...before she went home with her new family. I couldn't take care of her. My parents told me they wouldn't support us."

"How can you stand to be around them?" she asked suddenly irritated. "To live with them when they've been so awful?"

"They're not awful," I argued. "I don't think they under-stand. I know they love me. They fly me to California once a year to see Janet. They see the importance of me getting to see her. They just want what's best for me."

She looked unconvinced, but I knew there wasn't anything else I could say to change her mind. I thought for sure she'd understand the complicated relationship I had with my parents considering the struggles she and her dad had gone through.

"Mitch knows?" she asked, changing the subject.

I nodded.

"And he freaked out?"

Another nod from me.

"Oh, Gwen. I'm so sorry," she repeated the words she had said prematurely.

"Thanks," I said. "I've never been able to talk to anyone about this."

"Never?"

"My parents told me not to."

"Then tell me more about it," Katie said.

So I did.

I spent the rest of the afternoon talking about Janet, about the adoption process. I shared the pain I felt from placing her into another home, but the joy I experienced knowing she was loved so very much.

Katie listened and encouraged me throughout it all. Never faltering in her support, in her love. It was the first time since leaving California that someone other than Janet's parents respected my decision. Katie was very vocal on this point, and I was so thankful for her.

As our conversation continued, my heart slowly caught up with what my mind already knew. Every smile and every hug Katie gave me broke down a new wall.

I'd been fighting my emotions on this for years, so I knew one afternoon with Katie wouldn't fix it all. However,

I also knew this was a turning point in my life. I could allow the battle between what I knew to be true and what my family told me to be true wage on. It was a battle I was losing. Or, I could listen to my heart and find peace in the choice I made so many years ago.

That day, I vowed not to be ashamed.

I vowed I would fight until I only found joy in my decision.

CHAPTER TWELVE

MITCH

"MITCH BARBER, YOU ARE AN ASSHOLE."

Katie stood before me looking more furious than I'd ever seen her before. She was practically a foot shorter than me, but she made up for it with sheer tenacity. I was completely unprepared for such an assault to be brought down upon me.

When she had asked to come over, I figured it had to do with the recent accident. Her dad helped me make sure I got my truck towed after the accident, and had been helpful with everything. I thought this was a continuation of that.

"Katie," I said in a weak attempt to placate her. I lifted my hands and held them out toward her, the way you would approach a wild animal. She was definitely acting like one.

"You don't get to talk. You get to listen. And, if you're really lucky, I won't call Julian over to kick the crap out of you. Do you understand?"

She looked at me waiting for an answer, so I nodded. I wasn't sure if Julian would do it, but I had seen the dude wrestle back in high school. I didn't want to take my chances.

I wouldn't win that one.

"Gwen is one of the most gentle souls I have ever met. She befriended me when I was new to town, even though I was a hot mess. When I ran away to Florida last November, she forgave me for abandoning her."

"You don't understand," I argued.

"No, *you* don't understand."

"She lied."

"You didn't give her a chance to explain," she yelled at me. I watched as Katie closed her eyes taking a deep breath while squeezing her fists together a couple of times before she started again, calmer this time.

"Look, I get it. This has been a hard week. The accident, the scare with your sister, finding out that Gwen has a daughter in California. But seriously, you do not get to be angry with her about it."

"Aren't you even a little upset about the secrets she's kept?"

"If you knew the way her parents made her feel about it, you would think you were supposed to be ashamed too. If you'd been told the things she's been told, you would keep your mouth closed too, afraid to let anyone know."

"Well, I think it's great that you can get over it. I can't."

"Why not? You love her."

The words weren't a question. They weren't an accusation either. It was a statement of fact more than anything else.

"Love isn't everything," I said, refusing to admit—or deny—her words.

Katie stared at me, the fire back in her eyes. She didn't speak for what seemed like an eternity, and I felt myself start to fidget beneath her gaze. When had everyone decided they hated me?

"Mitch, you have a lot to think about right now. I hope you figure it out and I hope it's quick because I don't think you should talk to Gwen again until you do."

It was what Gwen said to me before abandoning me at the coffee shop. Thankfully, Sam was able to come pick me up. "Did Gwen tell you to say that?"

"No, but if you care about her at all, you will leave her alone until you pull your head out of your ass." With those words, she left.

I watched as she got into her fancy SUV and drove off. The same one I had been driving just a couple months ago. Everything was much easier then. I sat and watched as she turned off my street and out of view.

I was left sitting on my front step, freezing, too shocked to move for several minutes. In a matter of a week, I was jobless, truckless, friendless. Life had always been easy, and suddenly, everything was crashing down. It wasn't fair.

I wasn't a bad guy. I wasn't *the* bad guy everyone was painting me to be. So why did everyone keep acting like that? Everyone was pissed at me for one reason or another. I couldn't figure it out.

I worked hard to stay out of the drama that went around River Valley. I didn't consider myself part of any cliques when I was in high school, and I didn't fit into any now that those same people had graduated. I didn't spread rumors or add to the gossip. I liked everyone and liked being liked by them in return.

Except now I wasn't liked by any of the people I cared about.

I cursed to myself a few times before finally going back inside. I was going to need to find a way to get to my college classes while I figured out a new vehicle situation. It was safe to assume I wouldn't be riding with Gwen. It would still be a little while before my truck situation was sorted out. Sam had a car, but she was still in high school. She would need it and wouldn't be able to drive me out to Boise. I doubted she would want me driving it after everything that happened.

Damn it.

I started going through my mental list of friends. There were a lot of people I talked to. A lot of people who talked to me. Unfortunately, the more I replayed my interactions with different people, the more I realized I was a loner.

The thought took me by surprise. Loners were the weird guys who didn't have any friends. They wore trench coats and had greasy hair. They laughed at the most inappropriate moments. Loners were not the likable guy who didn't get too attached. Or were they?

Damn it.

Gwen was my best friend. Katie and Julian were friends by default. I didn't have many people beyond that. It was a painful epiphany to learn that I had a clique after all, and it only consisted of Gwen and me. Now that she wasn't talking to me, I was alone.

As I began a more intentional evaluation of my friend groups, there was one person that came to mind. She went to Boise State, lived just the street from me, and had a vehicle. Not only that, we'd known each other for what felt like forever. We'd grown up together.

Whether it was a deep seated friendship or just an acquaintance, it didn't matter.

The only hold up was I knew Gwen wouldn't be happy about it. Because the person who seemed to be my savior right now was one of the people Gwen hated most in this life. If Gwen knew about it, I knew she'd be disappointed.

I grabbed my phone and texted Michelle.

"I STILL CAN'T BELIEVE the wonder friends let you be seen with me," Michelle said to as I got into her sports car on Monday morning. She had agreed to let me ride with her to school but made sure I was aware that she would not be going out of her way to do it. She also didn't have a problem reminding me that she didn't approve of my other friends.

I didn't tell her the reason I needed a ride was because the so-called wonder friends and I were fighting. If she assumed so, she didn't show it. She just said she would let me ride along since we lived on the same street and left it at that.

I'm not leaving early or staying late. NO EXCEP-TIONS, her text to me read when I asked if I could hitch a ride. *I don't care if that means you're stranded at the school.*

I didn't have any delusions when it came to Michelle. While I didn't think she was nearly as awful as my other friends did, I was keenly aware that Michelle was Michelle's top priority.

"No eating or drinking in my car," she said running her fingers through her hair, looking at her reflection in the rearview mirror before pulling out of my driveway. "Oh, and you have absolutely no say in the music. So don't bother asking." With this, she turned on the radio to some cheesy pop song.

I don't know what I had pictured her listening to, but this wasn't it. It seemed too childish for the way she carried herself. I'd always imagined she'd listen to rap songs cele-brating a life of excess. Wasn't that the way she lived? Maybe some self-affirming chanting would be more fitting.

Definitely not the rainbow and sunshine crap she had blaring. I bit my tongue to keep myself from making a smart-ass comment.

We didn't speak the entire drive, and if she didn't remind me what time she was leaving campus, I would have thought she'd forgotten I was there altogether.

I wasn't exactly embarrassed to be seen getting out of the car with Michelle for several reasons. Least of them being, I don't think anyone would care or notice who I rode with. This wasn't high school anymore. I doubted anyone took notice.

Of course, it was the idea of that one person seeing me that made those uncomfortable feelings arise in me. I looked around hoping to get out of the parking lot and to class quickly. I'd be early, due to Michelle's schedule, but at least I'd make it to all of my classes today.

I forced down the guilt that threatened to rise as I kept an eye out for Gwen. I had nothing to feel guilty about. I was not the one who lied. I was not the one who kept a huge secret from my best friend. I was not the one who overreacted and threw a hot drink at my friend.

And yet, it didn't matter how much I told myself these things. Those unpleasant feelings still pushed back telling me I wasn't blameless. My feelings were wrong.

I went to my classes and tried to focus on my professors' lectures. I found it difficult to focus on any given day. Being one student in a sea of a hundred or more, I always felt like I didn't need to be there. I was always being overlooked. At home. At class. With Gwen. My thoughts wandered to that brown haired girl once during my class.

Okay, maybe two or three times.

Not more than four.

I didn't bump into Gwen on campus. I knew the best

way to make sure I accidentally found her between our classes. This meant, I also knew the best way to avoid her. I wondered if she made it to her classes today and was only slightly tempted to check.

When it was all said and done, the day went pretty well, and I managed to meet Michelle at her car just as she got there. I wouldn't be left behind on the first day of our arrangement.

"I suppose you're going to want a ride again tomorrow," Michelle said as we both got into her car.

"Yeah, I was hoping our schedules match up."

We went through our classes together on the drive home, and it turned out I would be barely late to my first class on Tuesday if we kept this arrangement throughout the week. I would have more time sitting around campus than I was used to, but it was a price I was willing to pay while I got my truck situation figured out. I hoped it wouldn't take too long to get a replacement.

In the meantime, I was thankful for Michelle. She didn't expect me to entertain her or pay for gas or anything. Her only condition was she wouldn't go out of her way. To me, it was a perfect compromise.

"Until tomorrow," I said to Michelle as she pulled up in front of my house.

She looked at me from across the front seat, not bothering to say anything. Her face was turned toward me as l I got out. I wasn't sure if she was watching me behind those dark tinted glasses, or sensing my fear like some wild predator.

I pressed my lips together hard to stop the laughter that threatened to spill out at the thought. It wouldn't do me any good to make her think I was laughing at her. Michelle expected everyone around her to have a certain level of awe in her presence.

"Thanks again," I managed to say with an even tone before getting out of her car and walking to my house.

It was going to be a long week.

CHAPTER THIRTEEN

GWEN

I STARED down at the phone in my hands.

Tuesdays were mine and Mitch's day. Who was I kidding? Every day was mine and Mitch's day. Avoiding each other for so long was killing me. I half expected him to come talk to me the night we fought. I still hadn't heard a word from him.

Isn't that what I told him I wanted?

No, I wanted him not to judge me. I wanted him to accept my past with open arms. I told him not to talk to me until he could do that, which meant he hadn't been able to get past it and was doing exactly what I asked him to do.

Then why was it so painful?

I had been staring at my phone all morning debating whether or not to call or text him and see if he wanted a ride to class today. I wasn't sure if or how he made it to campus the day before. Guilt over not helping him made my fingers itch to text him. I wanted to see if he needed a ride. I wanted things to go back to normal.

The other part of me wanted him to come crawling back. No, that wasn't it either. I wasn't so vindictive. I threw my phone on the bed in frustration. We went from best friends on the verge of a romantic breakthrough to complete silence between us. I couldn't come to terms with it.

My mom's voice shook me from my thoughts. "Honey, I think it's time we talked about the other night, don't you?"

I looked up to see her walking into my room. She made herself very comfortable and didn't even attempt to give me the illusion of privacy. I had no locks, and she didn't always knock before entering. I would love for her to at least pretend she was waiting for my permission before stepping into the only place I thought of as mine.

"Didn't we already talk about it?" I asked confused.

After getting the lecture about not ruining my life again, my mom hadn't spoken another word to me. I had assumed we were done with it.

"I wanted to give you time to think about what I said. You need to be careful about choosing your friends." She sat down on my bed.

"Wait. Is this about Katie?" She made it no secret that she wasn't a fan.

"I don't think she's a good influence on you. She is respectful to your father and me. That is the only reason we tolerate her coming over."

"Yeah, well she's been coming over less and less."

"Exactly. She's very impulsive. You don't meet the love of your life at eighteen. But she thinks herself in love, and you are put on the back burner."

"It's not like that."

"If you say so," she said skeptically, but quickly moved on. "I didn't come in here to talk about Katie though. I'm more concerned about your relationship with Mitch."

Just hearing his name hurt. "You'll be happy to know Mitch and I aren't dating. We're not even friends anymore."

"Really?" Her voice barely contained the excitement I knew she was feeling.

I hated her for it. I wanted to hurt her and said the first thing I could think of. "Really. You can rest easy knowing I'm not going to get knocked up again."

"Gwen." Her hand flew to her chest. "What has gotten into you? You cannot speak to me that way."

I wanted to yell at her—to say I could, in fact, speak to her that way. I wanted to lock her out of my room and tell her to never speak to me again. If I did those things, I had no doubt I would be packing my bags and looking for a place to live sooner than I had planned.

I didn't make a lot at The Farmhouse. It paid the few bills I had and gave me enough left over to have a decent savings. Living on my own would drain that money faster than I would be able to replenish it. I would be doomed to fail.

My mom probably knew that. Maybe she counted on it.

"You're right. I'm sorry," I said even though my heart wasn't in it. The words were enough to placate her. I watched as her face relaxed and her satisfied smile returned.

"Good. Now we can talk about this reasonably. I can't say I'm disappointed to hear about you and Mitch. Honestly, how could you not see the similarities between him and Ethan?"

It always went back to that. "They're not the same," I argued quietly.

"Oh, Gwen." My mother looked at me with pity. *Pity.* "Boys only want one thing. You found that out the hard way with Ethan. I didn't think you would still be so naive."

"Not all guys are Ethan," I said, my voice more confident this time.

I had a sudden moment of clarity and wanted to stand

firm without setting her off again. Mitch wasn't like Ethan. As much as that fear had driven me these past several months, I knew it was unwarranted. Oh, he could be an idiot—and we would need to address that—but he wasn't cruel.

I bit my tongue to keep from adding some comment about Dad only wanting that one thing, feeling recklessly bold in my new knowledge. It would be in everyone's best interest if I didn't show the flaw in her logic.

I could see by my mother's facial expressions she had her own internal debate going on in her head. She was trying to decide just how stupid her daughter was and if she'd have to worry about another unplanned pregnancy in the immediate future. Mercifully, she came to the same conclusion as I did and kept her mouth shut.

We'd leave it be—for now.

"Well, I'm glad we had this talk," my mom eventually said, even though we both knew she didn't mean it. "Don't you need to get going to class?"

I looked back down at my phone and saw it was time to go. My mom's little pep talk had decided for me whether or not I was going to pick up Mitch. I didn't have time now. The good thing was, the talk also forced me to realize it was ridiculous to always push him away.

Maybe he needed a chance to digest the news I dropped on him. Maybe he would admit he overreacted. We could make up, and I could finally admit my feelings for him. My optimistic attitude made the drive go by quickly.

I had two classes on Tuesdays and took the usual route walking from one to the other. It wasn't the fastest or most direct, but it meant that I would see Mitch. I wanted to see him. I didn't want to see him. My nerves were a jumbled mess that all congregated in my stomach. I felt like I was going to spew that mess all over the pavement if I wasn't careful.

This was Mitch, why was I so nervous?

I walked slowly as I passed through the hall in which we usually met. I didn't see him no matter how many times I turned my gaze from side to side. The guilt from not picking him up threatened to resurface. I shoved it down and quickened my pace to get to Spanish.

I hated Spanish.

I wished I had taken it in high school to knock out credits by doing AP classes. I wasn't very good at speaking it, and the fact that I couldn't roll my r's made it difficult for my classmates to determine if I was saying *dog* or *but*.

Today, we were conjugating verbs. The word *amar* was drawn on the whiteboard in the front of the class. *To love*. My answering growl was loud enough to catch the attention of the people sitting near me. It was like the universe was out to get me.

Amo. Amas. Ama. Amamos. Aman.

I love. You love. He loves. We love. They love.

I was already feeling like a poor lovesick girl with all my emotions running wild from this morning's revelation. This was all I needed. It might as well have been *Amo Mitch*. Maybe I could write the words on my notebook and cover the rest in little hearts. In large print, I could write *Mrs. Gwen Barber*. I felt like I was in high school—better yet, middle school.

I didn't want to look at the words, or *think* the words, or *say* the words, or even *hear* the words. I loaded up my stuff and walked out of the room even though I'd only been sitting down for a couple of minutes. The fantastic part about taking college courses was that no one tried to stop me.

I wasn't ready to go home yet. Despite my inability to sit in Spanish and conjugate love, I knew I wanted to see Mitch and talk to him. It just so happened it was one of those instances that a text wouldn't work. I wanted to see his stupid face. I wanted to watch those stupid dimples when he smiled.

The campus was lacking in the coffee department, but there was a healthy café that had great smoothies. Smoothies were only a small step from ice cream. Despite the frigid temperatures outside, ice cream solved all of life's major problems. Maybe a banana nut crunch smoothie would do the same.

The place served lunch, and there were quite a few students getting food. Ordering a smoothie in the dead of winter earned me a raised brow from the girl at the counter. I knew I couldn't be the only person who wanted one so I ignored it and found a seat.

I sat and attempted to study while enjoying my drink, but after an hour of letting my mind wander, I decided it was time to head home. It would be the perfect time to head toward the parking lot if I wanted to catch Mitch. I had barely touched my smoothie but brought it along with me anyway.

I walked quickly across campus to the parking lot. Between nerves and my brisk pace, I was breathing heavily when I caught my first glimpse of him.

He was dressed nicely—as usual—and his hair was expertly messy. Even without those markers, I would have recognized his walk. That was the strut I'd been looking for all day. Seeing Mitch opened the floodgate of emotions I'd been struggling with the last few days.

I loved him.

I hated him.

I wanted to run up to him and wrap my arms around him.   *↑ opposite feelings*

I wanted to throw my smoothie cup at him.

I followed him a safe distance behind, not calling out, wanting him to spot me naturally. If I had to call out his name, it would affect the response I so badly wanted to gauge. I didn't want him to have a chance to school his features. I wanted to know exactly what he felt toward me. Was it anger? Would he be relieved when he saw my smile?

What I wasn't prepared to see was Michelle walk up beside him and offer him a small smile. In terms of smiles, it wasn't much. But Michelle was like a different species. She was an evil, blood-sucking creature with talons to boot. I don't think I ever saw her look that happy to see anyone. Did she light up that way when she dated Julian? Why was she giving that look to the guy I was in love with?

You've got to be kidding me.

My steps quickened so I could pass him, throwing all original plans out the window. I wanted him to know I saw him. I knew I was acting like a jealous ex-girlfriend. I felt like a jealous ex-girlfriend, and I didn't care. I couldn't imagine making things any worse between us than they already were.

I walked by him casually bumping into him as I passed by. I didn't bother apologizing or looking at him as I left him and Michelle behind me. I made it to my car, too cool to care about what he did now that we weren't friends.

It was only when I turned the key in the ignition that I finally allowed myself to cry.

CHAPTER FOURTEEN

MITCH

"YOU KNEW SHE WAS BEHIND US," I said to Michelle when we got into her car. My first instinct was to chase after Gwen, but I wasn't sure if it would make things better or worse. I also wasn't sure I was ready to talk to her.

Michelle shrugged from the driver's seat and looked down at her long, red nails.

"Why?" I demanded when she refused to acknowledge me. She had deliberately given me a coy smile when she walked up to me. I'd been confused about Michelle's attention for only a few seconds before Gwen had bumped into me, shedding light onto her behavior.

"Call me a romantic," she answered flatly.

It was official. The female race was worse than I'd ever imagined—one hundred percent insane. They were most definitely living in their own little world, making up rules as they went.

"Romantic?" I asked, skepticism lacing each syllable.

As Michelle started her car and the heat from the vents began to warm the air, she turned to face me. "I know you and the friends for social justice–"

"I thought they were the wonder friends," I interrupted.

"Call yourselves whatever you want. I really don't care," she said impatiently before going on. "I know what you think about me."

"What are you talking about?"

She lifted her hand up toward me. "Save it. I'm not an idiot. What I was going to say is, I'm aware of the little groups that run around River Valley. I know you and Gwen have been dancing around each other for months. I thought a little jealousy would speed things up. So, yeah, you can call me a romantic. I'll admit, even I didn't realize it would go so well though."

"That wasn't jealousy. That was hatred. We're fighting."

"You're always fighting."

"Huh?"

"Yes, Mitch, I'm well aware of that part of your relationship too."

"Should I be worried you're stalking me?" I asked. It was weird that Michelle knew so much about me.

Michelle started laughing. "Please. As if I'd ever stoop that low."

"Okay, so why do you know what's going on?"

"I just know," she said cryptically. I waited for her to elaborate, but she didn't say anymore.

We sat in silence the rest of the way home with Michelle's pop music playing in the background. She didn't sing along, didn't hum. Even her fingers stayed unnaturally free from tapping along to the beat. I wondered why she listened to such upbeat music. It didn't appear as if she enjoyed it at all.

When we got to my house, Michelle stopped the car and smiled at me. Not the flirtatious smile from earlier, but a real smile. I couldn't remember the last time I saw an expression so genuine on her face. Not since we'd been children who played together on the same street.

As we got older, Michelle became more closed off. She was the school mean girl, and I was the loner. Gone were the days of riding our bikes around the neighborhood. Sometimes, it was easy to forget those days ever happened. But now every time I saw her, it was becoming easier to talk to her. Even in these few car rides, I couldn't help but wonder if my opinion of her had been marred by the people I surrounded myself with.

THE NEXT COUPLE of days went the same. Michelle continued to pick me up and take me home from class. Her pop music played in the background as she sat stoically. We began talking more and more.

"You never said why Gwen hates you," Michelle said on the ride home Thursday afternoon.

"It's a long story."

"It can't be longer than the drive."

"Good point. I guess I should say it's personal."

"Which means you're not going to tell me."

"Sorry." I wasn't really. It just seemed like the right thing to say after denying your chauffeur what they asked for.

She didn't push it, but it turned out that I had spoken too soon when I thought conversation was getting easier between the two of us. My refusal to go into what was going on between Gwen and me shut down everything.

I tried to start a few conversations after that. Each time, Michelle gave one-word answers, if she even responded at all. I gave up and leaned back in my seat, resigning myself to the music that was playing. When the song changed, I cringed. It was the song I sang to Gwen the night of the party.

"Michelle, please change it."

"You know the rules," she answered.

"Change the song," I repeated more forcibly.

Something in my voice must have indicated how upset I was because she turned the radio off. Things only felt more awkward now that we were riding together in silence. Not to mention the way I flipped out at the music.

"Ugh. I can't believe I'm even suggesting this," she said.

I looked over, startled by the way her voice broke the stillness inside her car. She looked physically pained by whatever she was about to say.

"Hang out with Avery and me tonight."

"What?"

"You heard me, Mitch." She sighed.

"Why would I do that?"

"Because your pep squad is acting like a bunch of dicks and you need cheering up."

"My pep squad?"

"Gwen, Katie, Julian." Her voice caught for a split second, over so quickly I wouldn't have noticed if I wasn't as focused on her words as I was. "Something is going on between you and your friends. Do something with us instead. Plus, Aves is super hot."

"I thought you wanted to hook me up with Gwen," I said wondering like hell what went through Michelle's mind on any given day.

"I changed my mind. Besides, it's just...whatever. Stop being dumb and come."

"Fine," I relented as she pulled up to my house. She

rolled down the passenger side window as soon as I got out and shut the door.

"Good. See you at seven," she said and pulled away before I could argue.

It was only after I made it inside I remembered what day it was.

It had been ages since the last time I missed one of Gwen's Thursday night shifts. If I didn't count Thanksgiving or any other major holiday, I had only missed one when I was sick in bed with the flu. Even then, Gwen had brought over soup for me after her shift.

To miss one of our dates would draw a line in the sand. It would send the clear message that things were broken between us and suggest we might not recover from our latest fight. I wasn't sure if I felt that way and tried to convince myself it was only a meal.

It wasn't as if I was cheating on her. We weren't dating. I wasn't dating Michelle or Avery. Except Gwen had a personal vendetta against Michelle. If she saw me with her, she would flip out.

I went back and forth on whether or not to cancel the entire afternoon. I knew that it would kill Gwen, but I reminded myself that I was angry with her. I had every right to be. She had a daughter in California. Gwen moved here a couple of years ago, which meant that she'd been keeping this secret from me for years. I wondered what else she was keeping from me.

I wanted to know Sam's opinion, so I knocked on her door. "Sam, open up."

The door swung open, and my sister stood before me, a scowl on her face. "What?"

"I'm having a bit of a dilemma, and I thought you might help me out."

Her eyes narrowed. "Are you serious? Did you know I'm grounded indefinitely because of what happened at the hospital? Jake won't talk to me. The rumors have already started spreading around school. My life is ruined, and you need my help?"

"When you put it like that."

"Mitch, you need to figure whatever it is you're struggling with by yourself. I don't have time for it." She shook her head and shut the door without giving me a chance to argue.

Ever since the bizarre breakfast after my accident, Sam had been acting weird toward me. She wasn't necessarily hostile, but she didn't want to talk to me like she used to. I went downstairs and found my mom in the kitchen making dinner. She was chopping peppers and onions for some pasta dish she liked to make.

"Hey, Mom." I hopped up on the counter beside where she was working.

"You know I hate it when you sit on the counters," she said without looking up from her prep.

"But you love me."

"What do you want, Mitch?" she asked as she wiped her hands on a towel and looked at me.

"I just wanted your advice about Gwen."

A deep sigh. "Again? There will be a day when you figure out how to handle your relationship with her. I don't have time for this right now."

No, of course not.

It was always something.

Gwen and Sam were pissed at me. My mom too busy for me. If I needed help deciding whether or not I should go out with Michelle and Avery, this was my sign. At least they wanted to be around me.

"Hey, I think I'm going out for dinner tonight," I said to my mom as I jumped off the counter.

"You usually do on Thursdays, Mitch," she said already back at work.

"Right," I said too annoyed to clarify.

It was better to play dumb than try to explain. She didn't even bother asking how I was getting to the diner. She was focused on what she was doing, and that meant our conversation was superficial. She couldn't be bothered to look any deeper into the details.

I went back to my room, waiting to hear from Michelle. I didn't want to be near my family. I studied for a few of my classes, struggling to focus. I read the same page in my textbook three times before my phone buzzed.

Michelle: Come on loser. Let's go eat.

CHAPTER FIFTEEN

GWEN

"I LOVE when we work Thursdays together," Katie said, as we hung out waiting for customers to come in.

We both leaned against the counter that was near the kitchen. It was a small tabletop that sat four people with backless stools. Customers rarely sat there because it was awkward and so close to the kitchen.

It was a good place to stand when you wanted to look busy or to find a place where you weren't breathing down your tables' necks. I was thankful Mike had scheduled us to work together since I usually worked with Sarah on Thursdays. I would need her by my side if Mitch didn't show up.

The thought stopped me. It came to me without permission. Yes, Mitch came every Thursday night to see me at work. Even when we were fighting, he would come and eat. We might not talk the entire time, but it was the way he reminded me we wouldn't be angry forever.

I wondered if he would come tonight. Not only was he without a vehicle, which would make coming more difficult in the easiest of circumstances, but we were fighting worse than we ever had before. I was also sure I didn't help things with my stunt on campus earlier.

The night was busier than I could have imagined. Katie and I both ran around like crazy to keep up. I was thankful for the influx of customers. It meant I wouldn't be too preoccupied with Mitch. If I was busy getting new drinks for my tables, I couldn't watch the door. If I was busy taking an order, I couldn't analyze everything that had happened in the last week.

I was cleaning up after a couple that had just left when I saw him walk through the door. I didn't realize I had been checking the door despite working hard all evening. My body instantly relaxed. I hadn't realized I was so tightly strung until that moment. Just one glimpse at his face eased the tension I didn't even know I was carrying.

I took a deep breath. Thank goodness our friendship wasn't over. I wasn't sure if I could handle that right now. There were so many things left unsaid between us.

For some reason, Mitch was standing there instead of sitting down like he normally did. Maybe he felt unsure about where we stood. I hated that I made him feel that way. Seeing his hesitation killed me.

I started to walk toward the hostess stand but stopped dead in my tracks when Michelle and Avery walked in behind him. He'd been standing there for less than a minute. I waited, holding my breath, praying it was a coincidence. Why would he be here with them?

I reminded myself Mitch didn't have a car. He would have needed a ride. Everything suddenly clicked into place, and I felt embarrassed by my behavior earlier. They lived on the same street and grew up together. I hadn't been willing to give Mitch a ride to school. Without a vehicle of his own, I'd left him with very few options. Michelle had taken care of him when I hadn't.

Now, she was bringing him here so we could eat together. It was a sweet gesture that went against everything I knew about her. It was hard to see Michelle as a decent human being after the way she broke up with Julian, but if she was willing to do all this for my best friend, maybe it was time to reevaluate my stance. I considered giving her and Avery a couple of free slices of pie as a thank you.

I smiled as I walked up, feeling optimistic. This wouldn't be a night filled with our usual ease, but that was okay. Things were going to be okay.

"Hey, I'm the right half of the floor tonight if you want to grab a seat," I said to Mitch, who looked uncomfortable.

I couldn't wait to talk to him and to get everything worked out. Another pang of guilt hit as I saw the way he couldn't meet my eyes.

I grabbed two menus for Michelle and Avery, and led the girls to a booth in my section. I didn't think Katie would want to wait on them, so I would just double seat myself and let her have the next two tables that came in.

Mitch sat down next to Avery.

"It's not that busy anymore, you can have your own table," I said to him, confused about why he sat down with them instead of grabbing the empty booth that backed up to it.

Michelle shot Avery a look that made her snicker in response.

I looked expectantly at Mitch, who still hadn't moved.

"I came to eat with them." He looked up at me, and I couldn't read the emotion in his eyes. They weren't cold or unfeeling. And yet they lacked the usual warmth I'd come to expect.

"Here? Tonight?" My voice cracked with the two words, and I hated myself for the response.

"Michelle was in the mood for a burger." He shrugged.

"Of course she was." My voice was steady this time, but my face felt hot. I knew it was bright red from the humiliation I felt.

I stood before the table, managing to keep it together while they all placed their orders. Avery had a lot of questions about the menu as if it was so complicated. It was freaking diner food, not a fancy French restaurant. What was confusing about burgers?

She flipped her long blond hair over her shoulder as I told her the toppings for the Cowgirl burger, even though it was printed on the menu sitting on the table in front of her. She did know how to read, didn't she? When she shifted in her seat closer to Mitch, I wanted to scream. Instead, I kept my face blank as she finally settled on a chicken finger basket.

After everyone had ordered, I walked away as fast as I could without running.

"What the hell is she doing here?" Katie demanded as I walked into the kitchen. She had her hand on her hip, and it was obvious she was waiting for me to come to the back. She didn't clarify who she was talking about, and she didn't need to.

"I don't know."

"Why is Mitch sitting with them?"

"I don't know," I repeated, hanging my ticket.

"And why does Avery look like she wants to eat him up?"

"I don't know," I shouted at Katie so loudly it startled Frank, the cook who was working tonight.

"You okay?" he asked, stopping his food prep and

turning to face me. He was an older guy and had a daughter. The over protective dad in him came out whenever a customer was rude. I'd admit, if you didn't know him, his stature and tattoos could be intimidating.

"I'm fine, Frank."

"Do I need to *accidentally* drop some food before plating it?"

"I'm fine. It's fine. Everything is fine," I said in near hysterics.

Everything was not fine.

Not by a long shot.

One of my best friends—who I happened to be in love with—was here with another girl. I wanted to believe that Mitch would never be so cruel. Unfortunately, all I needed to do was look out through the small kitchen window that opened up to the dining area to see that it was true.

Michelle and Avery were laughing about something, and even Mitch cracked a smile. He didn't look nearly guilty enough. He surely didn't react the way I thought he should when Avery's hand touched his arm. Nor did he move away when she leaned in just a little closer as she smiled.

I silently questioned if it was too late for Frank to drop the buns, but knew I would never go through with it. There were many times I felt like doing something to difficult guests. So. Many. Times. But it wasn't right. You never knew who was having a shitty day and needed some grace.

Not that Mitch was getting any.

"Gwen, step away from the window." Katie grabbed my hand and pulled me toward the walk-in. "Don't let them see how upset you are."

"I'm fine."

"Gwen, you've literally said the word *fine* more times

than I can count since being in the kitchen. I hate to say it, but you're not fine."

"Why did he bring them here?" My vision was blurry as I refused to let the tears that filled my eyes fall.

"I don't know," Katie said, echoing my words from earlier.

"Michelle has no right being here."

"I know."

"Thursday is supposed to be *our* day, and he brought Michelle."

"I know."

"And Avery."

"And Avery," she echoed.

Katie hugged me and didn't say anything else. There wasn't anything else to say. This was the pivotal point in our relationship. It showed that we weren't meant to be together. Mitch would always choose the path of least resistance, something I knew. I had just hoped that I was different. He'd always made me feel special. It was why this betrayal hurt so much.

Katie eventually returned to the front of the house to take care of her tables, but she reassured me she'd check in with mine too. Everyone had their food, so it would simply be a matter of refilling drinks. She could handle it.

I continued to hide out in the kitchen. Frank wisely didn't say another thing to me while I stood away from the order window, staying out of view of my tables. He focused on finishing up mine and one of Katie's orders.

Unfortunately, he finished my order in record time, and someone would have to bring it out to the table. Knowing the history between Katie and Michelle, or rather Julian and Michelle, I didn't ask her to deliver my food to their table. Besides, if I didn't go back to the table for the rest of the night, Mitch would win. He'd see how much I was hurting. He'd see how much I cared for him.

"Didn't I order the cowgirl?" Avery asked as soon as I dropped her plate on the table.

"Nope. Chicken fingers."

"I remember you telling me about a burger."

"Yep, but then you settled on chicken."

"Are you sure?"

Avery wasn't the brightest one. The words were on the tip of my tongue, ready to tell her as much, when Mitch saved me.

"Aves." *Aves?* He put his hand on her arm, and I immediately wanted to slap it off. "You couldn't decide and got chicken."

"Oh, yeah," she answered after looking thoughtful for a few seconds. I couldn't tell if she was playing dumb for my sake, or if it was sadly the way she was.

"Anything else?" I just wanted to hide again, but also knew I needed to pretend that everything was normal.

Avery opened her mouth to speak again, but Mitch interrupted a second time to say everything was perfect and that they were fine.

Fine.

They ate their food and were mostly content while they were eating. It didn't make it any easier though. I was pretty sure it was the longest hour I'd ever spent at The Farmhouse. That being said, at least Mitch had the common courtesy to leave a good tip when they left.

I wondered if he had gone full-blown douchebag or just a touch. Maybe the fifty percent tip was an indication he wasn't a lost cause. Maybe it was his way to make himself feel better after what he'd just done. Regardless, bridges were burned. I was done.

I went through the rest of the night like a robot, doing the bare minimum to take care of the few tables I had after that.

"I think I need a change," I said to Katie when my last table left.

"What do you mean?" She watched me from where she sat rolling silverware in napkins for the next shift. I sat down across the table from her and started rolling my own. It was the last thing on our list of side work.

"I feel like I'm about to break. My parents are unbearable. Mitch is being a jerk. I wish I had the money to up and leave like you did. Except maybe I'd move to Florida and never come back."

"That was a huge mistake, and you know it."

When Katie had impulsively left after seeing Julian get into a fight with his brother, she'd almost screwed up their relationship. Now, they were closer than ever. The trip helped Katie sort through some issues she was going through at the time.

"But it gave you clarity. You had space to figure out what you needed."

"I promise it wasn't as great as you think it was. Don't you remember how mad you were at me?"

"I just don't know what to do."

Katie bit her lower lip and took a deep breath. "Okay, hear me out. I've been thinking about moving out into my own place. I'm nineteen, and I have the money. I've just been waiting to make sure I'm not going to turn into a total waste again. What if you moved in with me?"

"Wouldn't you rather have Julian move in with you?"

"Gwen, we've been dating for what, three months? I'm not even going there."

"I couldn't do anything expensive."

"So, that's the other thing. I have all my mom's money, so that isn't an issue." She was always pulling crap like that. That money was her solution to everything. I started to interrupt her, but she kept talking over me. "I don't want to live by myself. I don't need a roommate, I want one. I'd prefer it was you."

"I don't know," I said, still unsure.

"Come on. It's kinda perfect, don't you think?"

I raised my brows but didn't say anything.

"Okay. The circumstances are not perfect. Mitch is a jerk, and I hate that he's being like that, but even you can't deny the timing works out."

I studied her face and saw something more than just a desire to help me. It was the reason she was pushing so hard. "You already have a place lined up, don't you?"

Her face lit up with a bright smile and her work stopped. She had a dreamy look on her face. The same look she got when talking about Julian. "I do. It's not an apartment, but the cutest little house."

"And?"

"And what?" she asked, guilt lacing her tone.

"How long have you been renting it?"

"How do you always know these things? I swear you have a sixth sense or something."

"Or something." Katie was easier to read than a stop sign. "How long?"

"Just a month. I signed a six-month lease hoping to ask you soon."

I laughed at her presumption. "What if I said no?"

"I guess I would have had to man up and live alone. So I'm thrilled you said yes."

I hadn't technically said yes yet. I wasn't sure if she

knew that or was too excited to notice. "How about you show me first? We can go from there."

"Gwen, you're going to love it."

I wished I had her confidence.

We finished up the last of our work, making plans to go see the place Katie was already renting. No pressure or anything. It was strange. I wasn't as anxious as I thought I should be. Katie was my best friend. Right now, my only best friend.

Maybe living with her would be good for me.

Me: I'm excited about tonight.

LIE.

I actually had mixed emotions about going out with Avery. I'd gotten her number after dinner at The Farmhouse. We'd texted a few times before I got the nerve to ask her out. As soon as I hit send on the text, I questioned whether or not it was a good idea. Avery's quick response hadn't given me much time to second guess though.

Aves: I've never been to a piano bar. I can't wait for you to see what I'm wearing.

My mind started going in all kinds of directions. From prom dresses to more Jessica Rabbit style apparel, I wasn't sure what to expect. I looked in my closet hoping something would stand out to me. I settled on a dress shirt and khaki pants. If I threw on a tie, it could go either way.

It had been so long since I'd been on a date. I couldn't remember if I even had my driver's license at the time. I felt strangely insecure about every decision. I opened my closet again to look for a new shirt.

"Hey, Mitch," my sister's voice called from the other side of my door. "Can I come in?"

"Yeah," I answered quickly putting extra clothing away. I didn't need her to see what a girl I was being.

We'd made up just a few days after our big fight. Sam was easily one of the most chill people I knew. She didn't like to hold grudges. I wasn't sure she knew how. Once things had settled down, she told me we needed to talk. I listened as she told me why she was so upset. Real remorse over my treatment of her and everything that happened led me to apologize. Things had gone back to normal after that.

"So Avery, huh?" she asked as though we hadn't already discussed it.

"Yeah."

"And Gwen is just *poof* out of the picture?"

"I told you, I don't want to talk about it."

My sister sat down at my desk and started moving back and forth in my swivel chair. "I know. It just doesn't make sense how you went from a lovesick puppy dog to this." She waved her hand in my direction.

"Things change," I argued. "You're not with Jake anymore."

Sam stilled. "Jake was horrible. You and I both know that. Hell, you're the one who helped me to see him more clearly."

"Gwen's betrayal was a bit more subtle than his."

"You still haven't told me what it was."

"Why don't you ask her?" I snapped.

I was tired of thinking about it, and I didn't want to talk about it. I stared at my sister waiting. She didn't have a quick comeback and went back to twisting back in forth in my chair. I pulled out my phone and started scrolling through random updates.

"Well, I guess that's my cue to leave," Sam eventually said, and set her car keys on the table. "I hope you have fun tonight with *Aves*."

I ignored her sarcastic tone and grabbed the keys. "Enjoy meatloaf with Mom and Dad."

But she was already out the door.

"THIS PLACE IS CUTE," Avery said as we sat down. I had taken her to a place that boasted being the best steakhouse in Boise. It was the most expensive place I'd ever taken a girl. It irritated me that she called it cute. Of course, ever since Sam left my room earlier telling me to have fun, I felt like every little thing was driving me nuts.

I looked back across the table at my date in an attempt to cheer myself up. She was anything but cute. Avery was hot. She'd worn a small dress despite the chilly temps and paired it with sky-high heels. It was something Gwen would never be caught dead wearing. Her hair was straight and hung down to the low-cut neckline of her dress. It left nothing to the imagination. She flaunted what she had, and it made it difficult to keep my eyes focused on her face.

Thankfully, Avery didn't notice my wandering eyes. She was busy looking at the menu. A little furrow formed between her brows. Soon, she had her bottom lip between her teeth. The menu was pretty basic, and I wondered if she was also nervous about our first date.

"Do you know what you're getting?" I asked, finally dragging her gaze up to me.

"Probably a salad. I'm considering going vegetarian."

"And I brought you to a steakhouse," I mentally berated myself.

"It's okay. I'm still on the fence. Tough decisions." A corner of her mouth lifted in a sardonic smile.

"Is that why you look so torn?"

Avery closed her eyes as a blush covered her cheeks. "Yeah. That and this night seems so weird, right?"

I didn't disagree. We'd been out together for less than an hour, and I couldn't find the ease that existed between us at the diner or in our texts. "You think so too?"

"Do you feel an incredible amount a pressure to make it work?"

The girl had no idea. After so many strikes with Gwen, I wanted to hit this date out of the park. The awkwardness was disconcerting. I hoped if we could get it out in the open, we could move past it and have a good night.

"It's overwhelming."

Her smile got bigger with my admission. "I'm so glad it's not only on my end. It's like Michelle just knows how to keep things flowing, don't you think?"

"Michelle?"

"Don't tell me you didn't notice she likes to play social moderator."

I thought back to the other night. Michelle stayed mostly quiet during our meal together, only contributing when conversation lagged. She brought up topics she knew Avery and I would both want to talk about and then sat back and listened as we got into it. I wasn't even aware of her manipulation until now.

"I never thought of that," I admitted.

Avery straightened up in her seat. "Oh, she's so good at it. We've been friends for years now. I've learned to pick up on it when she's doing it. Even so, I sometimes don't realize what she's done until it's too late."

"Too late? You mean like ending up on a date with a particular guy?"

She bit her lip again. "No offense, but you aren't what I usually go for."

I clutched my chest and fell over in my seat. "Oh, my pride. You've wounded me, my lady."

She laughed, a bright and bubbly sound. "See? This is what I mean. I tend to go for the guys who are too cool to say *my lady*."

"Too cool?" I asked slowly, sitting back up.

"You know, the ones who care about what people think about them."

"Ouch."

She put her hand on her forehead. "I'm sorry. This isn't coming out like I wanted it too. Can I try again?"

I waved my hand at her to continue.

"Thanks, *my lord*," she said seriously before smiling. "I mean to say, I like this. It's different, but it's fun."

"Yeah?"

"Yeah. I'm just not always good at this kind of thing."

We sat there smiling at each other for a few more seconds before our waiter came back with our drinks. Avery surprised me by ordering a steak and potato plate. To hell with salads, she was going to embrace the restaurant's specialties.

It was nice. The evening had started roughly as we struggled to find common ground. Once we did, conversation flowed easily. We didn't argue over which superhero was the greatest, which time lord was the best.

Avery wasn't into all of that. I quickly learned she preferred sports, especially football. She was a cheerleader in high school. After watching so many games from the side-lines, she knew her stuff. I was never overly athletic, but I enjoyed watching games on Sundays. I could imagine the two of us curling up together on the couch with a bowl of chips. She could rest her head on mine while we rooted for our favorite team.

We shared a dessert after our meal. Avery protested at first but quickly caved. At one point, she had a little whipped cream on the corner of her mouth. It commanded my attention, and I couldn't look away until she licked it off.

I imagined if I went in for a kiss, Avery would respond. The sudden thought made it impossible to think about anything else. I wondered what her lips would feel like. I needed to know she wanted me, to know she wouldn't turn her head.

"Hey," I said just as she was going in for another bite. "Wanna get out of here?"

She set down her fork and smiled. "Sure."

I quickly paid our check so we could leave. We walked out to Sam's car hand in hand. As soon as we got there, I pulled her into me. I had to know.

The moment our lips touched, she responded just like I thought she would. One hand rested against my cheek while the other hand wrapped around the back of my neck. She wasted no time moving her mouth against mine. We bumped noses. My mouth closed as hers opened. We'd barely started before we quickly pulled away.

"Huh," Avery said easily, but her brows were furrowed again.

She didn't need to explain her response. I knew exactly how she felt. There was no chemistry between us. Not even a little. A bad kiss didn't mean the end of the world.

However, I had no desire to try again. I didn't want to learn how to kiss her. I didn't want to kiss her at all.

I'd wanted this kiss to feed my ego. Ego fed, I felt nothing else. Thankfully, Avery didn't either.

"Yep," I said, my pride only a slightly damaged.

Avery's lips pressed together tightly as her shoulder began to shake. Soon, her hand was covering her mouth and laughter spilled out from behind it. "That was so bad," she said between fits.

"You know how to wound a guy."

She punched me in the shoulder gently. "Oh, stop it. Like you weren't thinking the same thing when we stopped. I saw your face."

I had a hard time processing her words, although part of me knew she was teasing me. I was too focused on the small action before she started talking. The punch reminded me too much of Gwen. I'd been comparing her to Gwen all night, thinking Avery was better. I was wrong.

My mind kept going to Gwen because it was trying to show me what an idiot I was for going out with someone else. I kept thinking about Gwen because I was in love with her. It didn't matter that I had been a complete ass. It didn't matter that she had a daughter in California.

I just hoped it wouldn't matter too much when I confessed I kissed another girl.

Because now I knew for certain there was only one girl I wanted to kiss, and I would do whatever it took to make sure she forgave me for what I'd done. I looked at the girl before me all made up in her fancy clothes. It was a façade. I learned that much just from this dinner together. I didn't want to hurt her, but I had to tell her.

"I'm in love with Gwen," I blurted.

The laughter stopped. "I know."

"What do you mean?"

"I think I knew at the diner the other night. The way you kept looking at her while we were there."

"Then why did you agree to come out with me? Why did you let me kiss you?"

"I don't know. Michelle thought we'd be a good match and I wanted to find out."

"I'm sorry."

"Don't be. I really did have a good time tonight. Maybe Gwen won't hate me too much, and we can hang out sometime."

"She couldn't hate you."

"If someone kissed the guy I loved, I don't think I'd ever be able to be in the same building as her."

I sighed because Avery brought up another very real obstacle. I knew I had made some piss-poor decisions these last few days. I also knew I was very much in love with Gwen. Unfortunately, Avery assumed the feelings were mutual. In her own way, I knew Gwen loved me. I didn't know if it would ever reach romantic proportions, though.

"Gwen doesn't love me. Not like that."

"Of course she does."

"What am I going to do?"

"Well, first you're going to drive me home. Then you're going to figure out how to win back the girl."

CHAPTER SEVENTEEN

GWEN

KATIE SQUEEZED my hand as my parents made themselves comfortable on the adjoining couch. I couldn't stop the small laugh that escaped at the way my mom looked at the place where mine and my friend's hands met. Her fingers were laced through mine when we sat down.

You'd think getting pregnant would be enough evidence of my interest in the opposite sex, but the way she stared made me wonder if she was bracing herself for a talk that was vastly different from the one that was about to take place. My dad looked like he wanted to be anywhere but where he was and still hadn't met my eyes.

My mom brought her attention back to my face. "Okay, Gwendolyn, you have our attention. What is it that you wanted to talk to me about?"

"Both of you," I said quietly.

"What?"

"You asked what I wanted to talk to you about. I asked you both to meet with me."

She looked genuinely baffled by the comment. She probably was. My mother always took charge of the situation. My dad so often let her and I never understood why. For wanting so badly to stick to traditional family values, they struggled to follow it in their marriage.

I took a deep breath. Mentally criticizing them would not help me with this conversation. "I'm moving out."

My mom gave me a sly smile. "Oh, really?"

"Katie found this perfect place." I'd not seen it yet—except in passing—but my mother did not need to know that.

"Oh, Gwen." Her voice was sympathetic, even though I knew she was anything but.

"This isn't a bad decision," I reassured her. "I'm almost nineteen and in college. A lot of kids have their own places."

"I didn't say it was a bad decision. Those are your words."

"But you thought it."

"Did I?"

"Why are you acting this way?" I yelled.

My mother was acting insane. Wasn't she the one who said I should get my own place if I couldn't follow her rules? This wasn't even about that. I just needed a change of scenery.

"What has gotten into you?" It was the same tone she used whenever she wanted to end a conversation or gain the upper hand. It always worked.

"Nothing," I said, feeling small. I was ready to tell her I was sorry. I couldn't move out. I felt Katie's hand squeeze mine again. "I need you to be happy for me."

"How can I be happy for you? This is a huge mistake."

"It's not."

"Well, don't expect to come crawling back when your friend ends up pregnant and kicks you out. I haven't forgotten what people used to say about that boy she's with." I winced at the words. "And don't think we are helping you. You want to move out? Great, but you're responsible for yourself now. That includes trips to California."

Janet.

Her parents and I had worked out a contract for me to visit once a year. It was usually during spring break, which was fast approaching. We'd already bought tickets.

My parents had always been the ones to pay for my flights out to California. Usually, my mom would come with me, and we'd stay in a hotel together—even though we had family that lived in town. I don't think she ever got over the embarrassment she felt over my *indiscretion*.

"The trip is just a couple weeks away."

"Then I guess it's good that I purchased travel insurance."

"How am I going to get out there?"

"I'm sure you'll figure it out."

I turned toward my dad to see if I could find any comfort there.

He still refused to look at me. Whatever declarations my mother made, I knew he would support her.

"I'll give you two hours to pack." My mom's voice brought my attention back to her.

Two hours?

I'd assumed it was going to happen this week, not today. The confusion must have been evident on my face.

"What?" she asked. "You want to pretend to be a grownup? Consider the two hours a parting gift."

I looked to Katie. Her face was sad. She'd had her share of drama with her family, especially lately with her dad. Even so, I didn't think she'd ever been mistreated this way. I could tell she was fighting hard not to give me the look she referred to as the pity look. I was impressed by her determination. If the roles were reversed, I'd be crying for her.

As it stood, I refused to cry. I would not give that woman the satisfaction of seeing me break down.

"I guess I'd better start then."

I walked up the stairs toward my room knowing Katie would follow me. As I started grabbing the clothing out of my closet, I looked over to see Katie grabbing my jeans out of the dresser. I had a couple of totes in my room, but I hadn't grabbed any moving boxes. I hadn't thought I would need them yet.

"It's okay. We'll just make a few trips," Katie said loading her arms up with my clothing. "At least our butts will be super toned after so many trips up and down the stairs, right?"

I tried to smile. She wasn't making light of the situation —I knew that—but I couldn't force my lips to cooperate. Katie didn't seem to notice or care. She just started the trek down to her SUV parked out front.

We continued this for the next two hours. Larger items were loose in the back of her vehicle, while I secured smaller items in the bags I had. My parents made themselves invisible while we carried all my earthly possessions down the stairs, although I could hear one of the sports channels playing in the other room. My dad was dealing with family conflict the way he always did, by pretending nothing was wrong.

I didn't know what my mom was up to. I didn't care.

I gave my room one final glance. We'd spent the last hour and a half stripping it bare. All that remained was the bed and the dresser. I desperately wanted to take them with me. Unfortunately, they wouldn't fit into Katie's SUV. I also knew if I attempted to move them, my mom would crawl out from whatever hole she was hiding in to remind me that she bought them for me.

I grabbed the box that usually sat hidden on my closet shelf.

"Ready?" Katie asked from behind me.

I didn't respond but just followed my friend as she walked out of my parent's house.

"WHAT DO YOU THINK?" Katie asked as we got out of her SUV. She put her hands together in front of her and looked at me with wide eyes. She was forcing excitement that neither one of us felt. I was tired. I knew she had to be too.

I flung my arms out. "Does it even matter at this point?"

"I guess not, but please tell me you love it."

"I love it," I answered, though I might have enjoyed a cardboard box at this point.

"Yay!" She pulled me in for a hug and squeezed me so tightly I couldn't breathe.

"Do I get to see the inside?" I asked while trying to push her off of me.

"Oh, right."

Katie led me to the front door of the house that she'd been leasing in secret. It was a small two bedroom/two bathroom house on what appeared to be a quiet street. There was a short white-picket fence around the small yard. Right now it was barren, but I could see where flower beds had been marked off. When spring rolled around, I could plant flowers. Maybe there already bulbs beneath the surface waiting to come out and show their beauty.

I wasn't a gardener. I sucked at keeping plants alive. I wasn't entirely sure why the idea of flowers and planting seeds excited me. The only thing I could come up with was the new beginnings they would represent. I was starting fresh with my life. What better way to do it than by cultivating a garden?

"Okay, so I thought we could go down to the furniture consignment place in town and get a few couches, maybe a little dining room table," Katie said as she walked me through the common rooms. "Also, with all this tile, we'll probably want a couple of rugs to help with the sound."

"I can't afford all that."

"That's fine, we'll figure it out," she waved her hand as she kept walking through the house, never looking back at me.

"No," I argued catching her attention. My voice echoed in the empty space punctuating the point Katie had just made about the acoustics. "My stuff literally fits inside your vehicle. I have nothing to contribute."

"You don't have to worry about it."

"Of course I do. And I'm in no position to help."

"Gwen, I was planning on living here whether or not you agreed to move in with me. I would have to furnish it regardless. I'm just glad for the company." She took a few steps toward me. "Seriously."

"I don't want to be that person. The one who only takes. The one who never gives." Tears formed in my eyes. I debated trying to stop them as I had earlier, but instead gave in and let them fall freely.

It wasn't the furniture. It was everything. Katie knew that as she walked over and pulled me in for another hug. This time, she was gentle.

"Oh, Gwen, we'll figure this out. In the meantime, let me help. That's what friends are for."

"I'm just still so confused by what just happened. Why was she so angry? Why was she so cold?"

"If I had any clue, I'd tell you. I've never seen your mom like that before."

"I have. When I first found out I was pregnant and told her I was going to have the baby."

"I'm so sorry."

"Me too."

We didn't speak after that. Katie helped me carry my things to what was now my bedroom. It was empty, and the tile would be hard. Thankfully, I grabbed my thick comforter when packing earlier. I could make a faux sleeping bag until I could afford an air mattress. Maybe Mike would let me pick up a few extra shifts at The Farmhouse while I stocked up on the essentials.

At some point, Julian came over. He grabbed a few of my things and brought them into the house. It didn't take nearly as long to unload my belongings as it had to gather them. When we finished, they gave me my space. I looked at my pile of stuff.

Life sucked right now. There was no way to get around that. My mom kicked me out of my house for expressing a desire to move out. It seemed ridiculous to be upset when I was planning to do it anyway. I just expected things to go differently. I was still reeling over my mom's reaction, my dad's lack of action.

Oh, and I missed Mitch—so much more than I wanted to admit.

While Katie attempted humor to ease the pain of today's events, I couldn't shake the funk. No matter how badly I wanted to give into laughter, or even a smile. Mitch would have found a way to make me laugh. And if he didn't, the familiar romantic tension between us would have been enough to distract me from my current frustrations.

Why couldn't he have accepted my past? Why was he able to cozy up to Avery so quickly? Why did my parents have to be such jerks? Why was everything falling apart?

Why?

CHAPTER EIGHTEEN

MITCH

"WHAT ARE YOU DOING HERE?" Sarah greeted me as I walked into the diner. She'd been a timid thing when she first started working here. However, Gwen had worked her magic on her and earned her loyalty. Something that happened with everyone she met.

Everyone but me.

I had royally screwed up, and I didn't need the scowl on Sarah's face to confirm it. I was acutely aware of my selfishness these past couple of weeks. As it stood, it took me much longer than I had intended to reach out to Gwen.

I'd gone to her house a few days before, only to be told by her parent's that Gwen was no longer living there and no, they didn't have her new address. I could have called, should have called, but I didn't. I wanted to see her when I apologized—not do it with a text message. This deserved more.

"I need to talk to her," I answered Sarah, looking around for Gwen.

"She's not here."

"It's Thursday, of course she's here."

The girl before me crossed her arms over her chest and lifted her chin. A defiant stance that begged me to argue. I knew there was a girl code saying you had to cover for one another in situations like this. My sister had done it for other girls more times than I could count. What Sarah didn't know was this wasn't like all those other times. I was really and truly sorry. I just needed a chance to apologize.

I continued to look around the diner for Gwen, but I never spotted her. I did see Katie and the tattooed cook everyone seemed to love glaring at me from the kitchen window. I gave a tentative smile and small wave that earned me narrower eyes in response. Could they even see through the small slits they kept open? I knew I shouldn't be making jokes, not even to myself. I mentally berated myself as Katie stormed out from the kitchen.

"I swear on everything in the universe Mitch, if you do not leave right now, I will let Frank kick your ass."

"Isn't that how Julian got canned?" I answered frustrated I still hadn't caught of glimpse of the girl I came to see. I instantly regretted the words.

Katie pushed her lips together and slowly shook her head back and forth. "Oh no, you did not just say that."

"I'm sorry," I apologized quickly before changing the subject back to Gwen. "Where is she?"

"Home."

"Her parent's said she doesn't live there anymore."

"I never said she did." Her face was an unreadable mask.

"Damn it, Katie. Just tell me where I can find her."

"You do still have a phone, don't you? If you want to talk to her"—she leaned in and whispered in my face—"you could try using it."

"Don't act like you've never made a mistake."

For the first time in our little exchange, I watched as Katie's bravado faltered. Her eyes turned toward the ground, and her shoulders sagged slightly. "You know I have."

"People make mistakes all the time."

"I know that, Mitch."

"So help me."

"I shouldn't. You really hurt her."

"I need a chance to make it right."

She sighed before bringing her gaze back to my face. She looked tired. "I'm not even kidding when I say I will murder you in your sleep if you hurt her worse than you already have. You have no idea what she's been through these last few days."

I'd been absent for too long. I could only imagine how much I contributed to her heartache. But I hadn't been around the last few days which meant that something else was going on and I was completely out of the loop.

Katie pulled out her phone, her fingers moving quickly across the screen. Shortly after, my phone buzzed in my pocket. "Do not make me regret this, Mitch," she said before walking away.

I pulled my phone out and saw she texted me an address. I was going to see Gwen.

WHEN I PULLED up to the small house on Cherry Hill, I was surprised to see Gwen's car in the driveway. I knew that she would be at this address, but I was still coming to terms with her moving out of her parents' house as fast as she did. Gwen tended to play everything safe. I wondered what could have happened to make her act so quickly. I wanted to know my part in it.

I didn't dwell on it too much in case I lost my nerve. I was anxious coming here, unsure if Gwen would forgive my stupidity.

The front door cracked open before I could knock. In the small space, I could see her. Short, brown hair stuck up in different directions. The sight would have made me smile if not for the dark circles under her eyes and the expressionless way she looked back at me.

"Can we talk?"

She stared at me for a minute while I held my breath waiting for a response. Finally, the door opened wider, and she stepped aside. A clear invitation to come in. Reluctant, but clear.

"I stopped by your old house, but your folks said you'd moved," I said as I walked into her new home.

"I did."

"They didn't tell me where." I stopped and turned back toward her.

"I don't think they know or care."

How could her parents not care?

The girl before me was a shadow of the one I knew. I couldn't stand to see her like this. I had a lengthy apology and explanation mentally prepared. I'd practiced it several times on the drive over.

"Gwen, I'm an idiot," I spit out impulsively ignoring the rehearsed speech.

She exhaled a laugh. Not the joyful sound I loved, but something much sadder. "For sure."

"I was selfish."

"True," she replied without looking at me. We sat there for what felt like an eternity before she spoke again. "I lied to you."

"It doesn't matter. I shouldn't have acted the way I did."

"No, you shouldn't have," she said.

"I'm sor–"

"Are you dating Avery?" Gwen interrupted.

"What?"

"Aves," she said with mock cheerfulness. "Are you dating her?"

Her eyes pleaded with mine to say no. I wasn't dating Avery, but I knew this was the time to come clean about what did happen between the two of us.

"No."

A sigh of relief from Gwen.

"But I kissed her," I confessed.

A string of curses that would put any grown man to shame burst forth from her mouth.

"It didn't mean anything. I thought she might help me get over you. It didn't. I missed you." I rushed to get the words out before speaking in the best robot voice I could muster. "*Resistance was futile.*"

The corner of her mouth lifted. The start of a smile, but still not quite right.

"Mitch, I—"

"I'm sorry I responded the way I did. I was completely overwhelmed, and I freaked out."

"But—"

"And I shouldn't have kissed her, Gwen." I let out my own curse. "I shouldn't have, okay? It made me realize that I never want to kiss another girl. It's you. It has to be you because I'm completely ruined for anyone else."

Another long silence stretched between us. I said what I needed to say and I waited impatiently for her to respond.

"I hate this," she said.

"Me too."

"No, you don't understand. I hate that I feel this way

about you. You were too perfect before, and I was scared to let you in. I was afraid you'd break my heart. And now... now you've completely broken me, and all I can think about is when you almost kissed me in your truck." She closed her eyes before whispering, "I wish I would have let you."

My first reaction was to rejoice in those words. She wanted to kiss me. It felt like a victory. But the more I processed what she said, the more I saw it wasn't. Not really. I'd broken her. "I am so sorry for the way I've acted. For everything."

"I know."

"Gwen, I—"

"Can I trust you?" Gwen looked up at me with hopeful eyes.

"What?"

"Can I trust you?" she repeated.

"Yes."

She studied my face, and I refused to move. I let her continue her examination barely breathing, willing myself to stay still. It didn't matter how long she took. I knew I would stay that way as long as necessary.

One second Gwen's face was scrunched up in concentration, the next it softened, and she moved toward me. She was giving me another chance. I didn't deserve it. I didn't deserve her.

When her lips crashed against mine, I gently pushed away from her. "Are you sure? We don't need to rush this."

She let out a surprised chuckle. "I'd hardly call this rushing. I've been running from you for too long and refuse to do it anymore. I forgive you—I always will—but you'd better kiss me this instant."

"Yes, ma'am." I pulled her close, and I kissed her. I was too selfish to fight it.

It was everything I'd hoped it would be. She smelled like Gwen. The clean smell of soap and something I couldn't figure out filled my senses as I attempted to get even closer. Her hands were in my hair messing up the haphazard style that always took so long to perfect. I didn't care. I cupped her face in my hands as I deepened the kiss.

Our lips moved together in perfect harmony, almost as if we'd been kissing for years.

The only downside was the height difference. It made it difficult to stay this way. I wasn't ready to stop. I couldn't imagine ever wanting to stop now that I knew what I'd been missing all this time. I reluctantly opened one eye to look for her bed. How hadn't I noticed this when I first arrived?

I pulled away. "Where's your bed?"

A blush covered her cheeks as she turned her head toward the corner of the room. There sat a pile of blankets and pillows. No freaking way.

"You're not sleeping on the floor."

"I didn't have a lot of options."

"Why didn't you tell me? I would have figured something out for you."

"Between you being pissed about Janet and showing up to the diner with Avery, when was I supposed to ask you for help?"

"Gwen—"

She put her hands up stopping me. "Look, I forgive you. But that doesn't mean these past couple weeks haven't sucked."

"I can see that."

I didn't know what else to say. I hated that we could go from kissing each other to fighting all over again so quickly. My fingers tapped against my leg as I thought of what to do to get us back on track.

Gwen beat me to it. "I'm glad you're back."

"Me too."

"We have a lot we need to talk about." I nodded at that, not trusting myself to speak. "But I think that can wait until a little later," she said before dragging me to her makeshift bed and kissing me again.

CHAPTER NINETEEN

GWEN

I STILL WASN'T sure what to think about the day before. I'd been concerned I was slipping into a depression when Katie texted me.

Katie: You have about 10 minutes before Mitch shows up.
Me: Not funny.
Katie: Not kidding. Brush your teeth and put a bra on.
Me: Did you see him? Why did you give him our address?
Katie: I gotta go, it's super busy.
Katie: BTW, you probably only have 8 minutes now.

She was so full of it. Thursdays were rarely busy. They were one of my favorite shifts at the diner. Just enough business to make the drive worth it, but not so bad you'd end up scrambling the entire night. I was scheduled for my regular shift and needed the money, but asked Katie to cover for me just in case Mitch showed up. I didn't want to see him.

I'd been thankful for the night off until the texts from Katie came in. I felt betrayed by her. She knew how much

Mitch hurt me. How much my parents hurt me. I didn't think I'd be able to face him but ran around brushing my teeth and getting dressed in clean clothing just before I heard a car pull into our driveway.

It wasn't the sound I'd grown so accustomed to over the last couple of years. The old truck had an engine rumble I would recognize anywhere. When I looked out and saw a newer SUV, my heart sank a little. Part of me would miss the truck and the memories we'd shared together.

When Mitch walked up the sidewalk to the front door, I didn't pretend I didn't know he was there. When he asked for forgiveness and seemed genuine about it, I didn't hold his earlier actions against him. Even when he confessed to kissing Avery, I forgave him easily. The brokenness on his face was enough to tell me he regretted everything from the last couple of weeks.

And when he kissed me. Whoa.

I wanted to kick myself for denying him for so long. It was the kind of kiss people wrote songs or poetry about. It was finding the missing piece I never knew I'd been living without. It didn't take long for us to find our rhythm. It was so natural. In some weird way, it was like we knew what to do because we knew each other so well.

When we'd finally pulled away from each other long enough to admit we needed to talk, I was amazed at how smoothly it went. He never shifted blame or tried to run from his wrongdoings.

We'd just finished talking when I pulled out my picture box and showed him the pictures I'd wanted to share with him for so long. He smiled and asked me more. Against my better judgment, I even showed him the picture of Ethan and me. I kept it hidden at the bottom of my box of mementos. So many of the items I kept tucked away held a special place in my heart. That picture of us was the reminder to protect it.

"I want to punch him in the face," Mitch said as he looked at the photograph.

"You'd have to get in line."

"He's the reason we've missed out on so much time together."

"You could also say he's the reason you know me in the first place," I argued.

"So you're saying I should give him a big kiss instead?"

I laughed at the visual. "I should warn you he's a sloppy kisser."

A look of disgust filled his face, and I winced at his reaction. "I don't want to imagine you kissing this guy."

"I thought we were imagining you kissing him," I tried to joke, but Mitch wouldn't have it.

"Gwen," he said gently.

"Believe me, I don't want to remember it either."

Ethan had been a terrible kisser, always trying to swallow my face. But he was popular and cute and–

"Do you ever talk to him?" His question stopped my mental rabbit trail. I hated when Ethan invaded my thoughts. He wasn't welcome there.

"Not really. He was pretty clear about not wanting anything to do with Janet or me. I saw him once at a gas station while I was visiting. He refused to even look at me once he recognized me and drove off as soon as he was done."

I didn't say anything else for a long time after that. Neither did Mitch. Really, what was there to say at this point? Life was a mess.

He wrapped his arms around me, and I melted into his arms. He shifted, and I felt his lips press against my forehead. Then they were on the top of my head, never pushing for anything more.

I was disappointed. I was thankful. There would be plenty of time for passionate kisses, I hoped. Right now, I needed comfort, and he was doing just that with the innocent kisses he gave.

I leaned further against him but quickly found myself lying in his lap. I was just so tired. He ran his fingers through my hair soothing me. The movement over my scalp was heavenly. I closed my eyes, just for a minute.

That single minute turned to several minutes, and soon I was asleep.

I WOKE UP SLOWLY, lingering in the fog that sometimes came with waking. Sleep had overtaken me while Mitch played with my hair. Katie and Mitch were whispering in my room, so I kept my breaths slow and even. My eyes begged to look around, but I forced my eyelids to relax and kept them closed.

"What the hell happened with her parents?" Mitch asked after a minute of small talk.

"They were so awful. They kicked her out and gave her a time limit to gather her things."

"What kind of parent does that?"

"The kind that makes their child feel like crap when they choose adoption. It's a miracle Gwen doesn't have a major complex about the whole thing."

A long pause made me wonder if the conversation was over. I considered sitting up, but Mitch spoke just as I went to move. "I did the same thing to her."

"I think she knew you were upset. She's so good at reading people like that."

"It doesn't excuse it."

"No, but she forgave you."

"Thank goodness." There was another break in the conversation before he continued. "I kissed Avery."

It wasn't news to me, but it was still difficult to continue the charade at his confession.

"How could you? Does Gwen know?" she whispered angrily.

"Let's just say she can be very forgiving."

"Yes, she can. But take it from someone who has made some crappy choices in love. Don't mess this up."

Love.

I knew Mitch loved me just like I knew I loved him. I still wanted to hear him say it. I held my breath waiting for his response. As the silence stretched on, I started feeling guilty for listening in on their conversation. Mitch had the right to tell me how he felt on his own terms.

I made a show of sighing loudly and stirring. I stretched my arms above my head and blinked my eyes slowly a few times. The look Katie gave me as I turned toward her said she wasn't the buying the act. She knew me well.

Fortunately, when I turned my head to face Mitch, he only looked happy to see me awake.

"Hey," he said with a sweet smile.

"Hey," I responded with a grin of my own.

The thing was, I was happy to see him. The fact that he was still here when I woke spoke volumes. I hoped it meant I could trust him not to abandon me again. Sure, he'd freaked out when I first told him about Janet. That wasn't something I was willing to forget. We would need to talk about it more in depth, but I forgave him.

"Oh," Katie interrupted awkwardly. Mitch and I were still grinning at each other like idiots. "I totally forgot I was supposed to...um, call Julian right now. I'll see you guys later."

"Okay, see ya," I said catching her eye and giving her what I hoped was a look that said we would be talking about this—soon.

"Hey," Mitch said again once she'd left the room, bringing my attention back to him.

"How long was I asleep?"

"A couple of hours."

"What?" I sat up quickly. I thought I'd been asleep for maybe thirty minutes. To hear otherwise was jarring. Although, if my mind wasn't so fuzzy, I would have been able to piece it together since Katie had just been in my room and she worked my shift earlier. Even a quick peek at the window of my room showed it was dark outside.

It was undeniable the last few weeks had been exhausting, mostly emotionally. However, with the recent move and trying to pick up extra shifts, I was physically drained too. It made sense I slept for as long as I did.

"Calm down," Mitch said as he put his hand on my shoulder. "You don't have anything to do or anywhere to be right now."

I looked at him in confusion. How would he know anything about my schedule when he'd been missing from my life for so long?

He answered my silent question. "Katie told me. I texted her when you fell asleep. She just got back and was checking in on you when you woke up."

That made sense.

"Gwen, I'm happy we're talking and..." His voice trailed off, and I swore I could see a slight blush hit his cheeks.

I'd never really thought about guys getting embarrassed like that. I fought the urge to make him finish his sentence.

After eavesdropping on he and Katie's conversation, I had a good idea of what he was going to say. I waited for him to continue.

"What the hell happened with your parents? Why did they kick you out?" Not what I thought he was going to say.

"They didn't. I needed a big change, and they weren't ready for it." I stared intently at my fingers as they played with the blanket we sat on.

"You needed change because of the way I acted, didn't you?"

I couldn't answer right away. It wasn't exactly his fault —not really.

My relationship with my parents had been on a downward spiral for a long time. I think it started when I first found out I was pregnant. We'd never recovered. Mitch was simply the last straw in a series of several conflicts.

He took my silence as confirmation. "I'm so sorry."

"It's fine, really."

"I want to make it up to you. Let's go do something fun."

As if it was as easy as that. "I can't. I have so much crap to do."

"Take a day off."

"I gotta figure everything out, Mitch. I can't just get up and do whatever I want. Plus, money is no joke right now."

"It'll be my treat. Isn't that what boyfriends are for?"

"Boyfriend?" I asked confused.

I hadn't thought that far ahead when I kissed Mitch earlier. It was the logical conclusion, but it sounded weird coming from his lips. Those lips I'd just been kissing...

"Or whatever," he added quickly. "Like I said earlier, we don't have to rush anything. We can call each other whatever you want. We don't have to use titles or–"

"Just stop talking for a second." I put my finger up and closed my eyes. I needed to think, and his chatter was making it impossible.

Boyfriend.

Mitch wanted to be my *boyfriend*.

He wasn't proposing marriage. He wasn't asking for some huge commitment. It was just a word. A word couldn't hurt me. And yet, it was just one more way in which Ethan had ruined me. He was the only person I'd ever dated. I'd fallen head over heels for him, and he'd completely betrayed me when I needed him the most.

I hated this. My brain was telling me how stupid it was to hold his sins against Mitch. I could write a term paper on the many ways Mitch was superior to Ethan. That didn't stop my heart from hesitating.

"Gwen?" Mitch asked quietly. He'd sat silent for several minutes while I attempted to work it out. I looked up at him. His eyes looked sad, worried. He was biting his finger, something I couldn't remember ever seeing him do.

My mind went to the traveling siblings who came into the diner not so long ago. The sister, Char, had left a note urging me to be adventurous. With all the talk of their travels, I'd taken the advice at face value. I'd assumed she meant to travel like the two of them were. But I realized it could apply to this situation right now. I could be brave and adventurous with my relationship with Mitch.

"Yes."

"Yes?" he asked confused.

"Yes, you are my boyfriend. And yes, you are taking me on an adventure."

CHAPTER TWENTY

GWEN and I had spent quite a bit of time confirming our new found relationship status that night. I never wanted to stop kissing her. Even hours later, my lips raw, I would turn around and go back for more if she asked.

Unfortunately, she still had a lot of stuff to do to get settled. Not to mention her regular responsibilities at the diner and school. I reluctantly left and went home. I felt great. Gwen and I not only made up, but we'd taken our relationship to the next level.

Freaking finally.

We'd also begun planning out an adventure to a nearby hot springs resort. It was a couple of hours away but was supposed to be one of the best commercial places. I figured the drive would give us plenty of time to catch up and explore our relationship further. I also thought it could serve as a great test run for an idea that came to me that night.

Gwen had briefly mentioned her mom canceling their trip to California. It would mean she wouldn't get to see Janet. That didn't seem right to me. My older brother was living in San Diego, not too far from where Janet's family lived. I wanted to surprise Gwen with a road trip over spring break to see her daughter. I hadn't said anything to her yet but planned to research it when I got home.

When I walked into my house, I could see my parents and Sam all sitting on the couch watching an action movie they'd been talking about non-stop. Even Luke had texted me a few times about it. I swore I was switched at birth. It was the only explanation for how different I was from the rest of my family.

My mom and dad's eyes stayed glued to the television as I shut the front door. At least Sam had the decency to turn toward me and give a small wave. I didn't linger though. I had a road trip to plan. Two if you counted the surprise trip to California.

As soon as I got to my room, I went online and looked at the route to San Diego. The drive would take about fifteen hours. I assumed that didn't include gas and food breaks. Driving over two days would be ideal since I didn't think either one of us would want to drive that much in one day.

So I started looking for places to stay the night. We would be driving right past Las Vegas. I'd always wanted to go to the city of sin, see the bright lights on the strip. We lived so close but had never been. True, neither one of us was old enough to drink, but it would still be an exciting experience. The main hurdle would be convincing Gwen it was a good idea.

There were hundreds of places we could stop between here and California. Any one of them a better fit for the girl I loved. Still, I couldn't stop looking at hotels near Vegas. I wanted to go and didn't know if I'd have another chance soon.

I was so busy looking for places Gwen might approve of,

I didn't hear my sister as she walked into my room. "Hey, Mitch," she spoke softly from behind me. It was said innocently enough, and yet I still jumped out of my seat when I heard her. Sam thought it was hysterical. I was less amused.

"It's not funny."

"Of course it is. Anything that I can do to pay you back for the whole pregnancy thing makes me happy." Her tone was not unkind, and she wore an easy smile on her face.

She'd been doing that for the last few days. Making jokes here and there about the accident, about her ex. We'd made up, but I couldn't help but wonder if she'd actually moved past it or was using humor to mask deeper feelings. I knew I should push her to talk about it with me, but I had so much going on with my own life. I could not open that can of worms. Not yet.

"Poor Mitch never gets the love," I joked, going along with it.

"No? Then I guess things didn't go well with Gwen?" She said it as a question, but we both knew otherwise.

I smiled big. "It went well."

"Obviously. You were gone for so long I was beginning to wonder if you eloped."

"I considered it."

Sam laughed and sat down on my bed. "As if that would ever happen. Gwen's way too cautious for that." She tipped her head at my computer. "What are you looking at?"

"Hotels in Vegas."

"Holy crap," she yelled and immediately shot back up off the bed to walk over to my desk. The screen currently showed a hotel that boasted theme weddings. "Please tell me you guys aren't running off to get married."

Now, it was my turn to laugh. "No, we're not. We're only eighteen."

"We live in River Valley," she reminded me. "That's not so far off."

I lifted my right hand like I was reciting a pledge. "I am not marrying Gwen." After a quick pause, I added, "Not yet."

"Then what are you doing?"

"We're going to take a trip out to San Diego." She didn't know it yet, but I couldn't imagine her saying no.

"To see Luke?"

"Yep." Mostly true.

Her eyes narrowed. "Then why is Gwen going?"

"Why not? She's my girlfriend. We can take a trip together," I said, a touch defensive. If Sam noticed, she didn't mention it.

"Take me with you."

"We're going during our spring break, and yours is different."

"I'll skip."

"I doubt Mom and Dad would let you."

"I could say it's mental health after everything," she continued to push.

"Sam, I need it to be just Gwen and me."

"Fine." She huffed and went back to my bed. "So it went well with Gwen?"

"Yep."

"What did she say about Avery?"

"Obviously she wasn't happy I kissed her. But she was amazing and forgave me."

"And she's okay you're still friends?"

It probably wasn't fair to keep in touch with Avery while I was reconciling with Gwen. I'd confessed our short, and incredibly awkward, kiss. However, I'd failed to mention we were still talking. There was nothing but friendship between the two of us. Avery had helped me work through recent events and genuinely wanted to help me win Gwen over. She'd even found someone she was interested in, some guy in a local band.

There was nothing but friendship between us, but I still hadn't told Gwen. Gwen had guy friends. Surely I was allowed to have girl friends. She and Julian had been pretty close when they both worked together. I knew there was nothing romantic between the two of them. I didn't think they'd ever kissed, but that was beside the point.

"Mitch," Sam said when I didn't immediately respond to her question. "Please tell me you told Gwen you're still talking to her."

"Not exactly."

"That is going to come back to bite you in the ass. I guarantee it."

"Maybe," I said not entirely convinced.

"Gah!" She threw her hands up. "How can you be so dense? I swear, sometimes I don't know how you've managed to get any girl's attention, especially Gwen's."

"It's not that big of a deal. And besides, Gwen is so great about everything."

"Yeah, well even great girls have breaking points," my sister said sadly before leaving my room for the night.

CHAPTER TWENTY-ONE

GWEN

"I CAN'T BELIEVE we've never done this. Why have we never done this?" I asked from my spot in the hot springs.

There were plenty of places to find hot springs in Idaho. Some were off the beaten path and required hiking to get there. I'd seen plenty of friends post pictures online of their trips. It looked like fun, just not the type of fun I wanted to have. The idea of walking through the cold snow to get into a warm pool of water wasn't so bad. It was the thought of getting back out into the cold and walking back that turned me off completely.

I'd been told it was worth it, but I refused to try it for myself. I'd lived here for close to three years, and I'd never experienced the wonder of the springs. Feeling the warm water all around me had me hating myself for not doing it sooner.

"Seriously, this is like heaven." I closed my eyes and groaned as I sunk lower into the pool. It was better than any bath or Jacuzzi I'd ever been in.

"Okay, first of all, please stop making those sounds," Mitch said from his spot beside me.

I opened my eyes just enough to give him a questioning look.

"They're um...distracting." He made a sound that sounded like a cough. "Second of all, I told you so. I've been telling you for years this was where it's at."

"It didn't sound *this* good though."

He mumbled something under his breath about something else sounding good.

I didn't catch it all, and I didn't care. I was currently figuring out how I could live in this water forever. I could change all my courses to online classes and find a work from home job. I'd get a laptop that was waterproof so I could work poolside. Wait, did they even make those? I could invent them, and that would be how I funded a life of never leaving the hot springs.

"Gwen."

"Huh?" I answered lazily.

"You did it again."

"Did what?"

Mitch laughed at me and kissed my forehead. "I was just asking you how you would feel about another road trip."

"To another hot spring?" I asked eagerly.

"You're enjoying yourself, aren't you?"

"You have no idea."

"It's pretty obvious." He laughed again. "No, I was thinking someplace a little warmer. Maybe Southern California?"

That was enough to get my attention. Mitch's brother was going to school in San Diego, but that's not what I cared about, and he knew it. It was who lived just a couple hours from Luke that got me excited. Any grogginess I felt left as I listened intently to what Mitch was saying.

"Spring break is coming up. I know you originally had plans to go out and see Janet then. Now that you don't have a plane ticket anymore, what if we drove? I could see Luke while you see your daughter."

It was official. Mitch was beyond perfect. I couldn't help but see the similarities between him and the springs. I'd resisted them both for so long. Now that I knew better, I was never letting either of them go.

He didn't flinch when he said the words *your daughter*. He also didn't push to see her or meet her. I wasn't sure if it was because he didn't want to or if he somehow knew how inappropriate it would be. Either way, it was exactly what I needed.

"Are you serious?" I asked still unable to believe I hit the boyfriend jackpot. It shouldn't have surprised me. Mitch had been a great friend for years. It only made sense he would rock the boyfriend role.

"Can you get the days off from work?"

"I already did."

"When?" he asked, tilting his head.

"Ages ago. I never told Mike I was staying in River Valley over break. I was holding out hope."

"Then it's a good thing you have a knight in shining armor."

He really was my knight.

I looked around to make sure no one was nearby or looking in our direction. It wasn't busy, but I wasn't a big fan of making out in public. When I saw the coast was clear, I leaned over and kissed him. Not like the sweet kiss he'd place on my forehead earlier. I really kissed him, grabbing his face and pulling him to me. He kissed me back with the same fervor before pulling away.

"Seriously, Gwen. This is not the place." He coughed again. "But I'm glad you're excited."

"I didn't think I could love anything more than this place, but I think you just took first place."

I expected Mitch to make a joke, maybe something about him always being in first place. Instead, he surprised me by becoming very still and looking at me with a somber expression. "Do you?"

"Do I what?" I asked confused. We'd both been giddy, and the mood completely changed with his question.

"Do you love me?"

"Holy crap, Mitch. Don't scare me like that. I thought something was wrong." I went to push him, but he grabbed my hand.

"Tell me."

"What?"

"Please, Gwen. Just tell me you love me."

"Yes, I love you. I think I've been in love with you longer than I even realized. You've been my best friend since I first moved here. You're the one I go to when I need a laugh, the one I can trust with my secrets, even if I kept them for too long. You're loyal and patient, and you are my other half. So yes, Mitch Barber, I love you."

He smiled and winked. "I know."

It was the response Han gave Leia in *The Empire Strikes Back*. I'd made him watch all the movies with me, time and time again. For him to respond this way was a testament to his devotion. He didn't have to say he loved me back for me to know. I kissed him again before sinking back into the water.

This afternoon couldn't get any better.

We stayed at the springs for another hour before finally dragging our pruney butts to the showers and heading home. It was such an amazing trip, and I kept watching Mitch on the drive back. He would be the perfect road trip partner for the drive out to California.

"Wanna put on some music?" he asked, interrupting our comfortable silence.

"Sure, my phone is almost dead though."

I had maybe 5% left after spending too much time scrolling poolside. It was mostly research on waterproof computers, which did exist by the way. Which meant I'd have to find a different million-dollar idea. It didn't matter. I would find another way to live my life of leisure.

Mitch handed me his phone, and I turned it on surprised he had it off while we were there. A message immediately lit up the home screen.

I had a strict no texting while driving rule. Mitch was always gracious to follow it when he was with me, so I was used to opening up his messages for him. What I wasn't used to was seeing texts from people mysteriously referred to as A, especially not with my name in them.

A: Are you with Gwen? Can you talk?

Why in the hell was someone asking if I was around? The only person I could think of whose name started with A was Avery. Considering what happened between the two of them, I assumed it was her.

Deep breath. That didn't mean anything. I scrolled up a little to see what else this person was sending Mitch. I read the texts just above it.

A: How'd it go?
Mitch: Good. I kissed her.

A: Not better than me I hope.

Mitch: I don't think any kiss could ever top THAT.

A: A kiss to remember!

He'd told me that kiss made him realize how much he needed me. He reassured me nothing was going on between the two of them. These texts said otherwise. Not only did they kiss, but apparently it was the kind of kiss you never forgot.

"Can't find anything good?" Mitch asked pulling my attention from the devastating exchange on his screen. He wore an easy smile on his face. It was just like what happened with Ethan. A charming smile always had a way of hiding everything else.

I was the biggest fool on the planet. Forgiveness came easily to me. I'd been so happy to hear Mitch tell me he was wrong; I didn't think to guard my heart.

He kept talking. "We could always play your favorite song. I know how much you love–"

"Are you still talking to Avery?" I interrupted.

"What?"

"You got a text from her."

Mitch didn't answer right away. The road we'd been driving down was a mostly deserted two-lane highway. He quickly pulled the car off to the side, unbuckled his seatbelt, and faced me. The expression on his face told me everything I needed to know.

"How could you?" I asked before he had a chance to say anything.

"It's not what you think."

"What do I think?" I asked, and smacked my hands against the center console.

"You think something's going on between the two of us."

"Wrong. I'm thinking I'm an idiot for kissing you after you admitted to kissing her."

"I told you it meant nothing."

"Then why did you change her name to A? Why is she asking if it's safe to talk? It seems like you have a side chick or whatever people call it." I pushed the heels of my hands against my eyes. I wasn't crying. I was just so, so sick of it all. "Am I the other woman—or the original too blind to see what was going on?"

"Gwen, please give me a chance to explain."

"I did give you a chance. I gave you a chance, and you screwed it up. Now it's too late. This is on you, Mitch." I leaned back in my seat. "Please just take me home."

I waited for him to argue, to push it further. I should have known he wouldn't. That wasn't Mitch's style. He sat quietly for a minute or two before sitting back in his seat and putting his seatbelt back on. After that, he drove me home without another word.

He drove me home without fighting for me.

CHAPTER TWENTY-TWO

MITCH

GWEN WAS RIGHT. I was an idiot.

I couldn't seem to get anything right these days. My parents were still weirdly distant. I wasn't sure what I did to mess that up, but at this point, I was sure it was my fault. Gwen, Katie and even Julian refused to talk to me.

I finished my last class and was officially celebrating Spring Break, not that I had a lot to celebrate or a lot of people to celebrate with. I was all alone—again. Only this time, it was worse because I couldn't see ever getting Gwen back. I'd been insensitive about Janet. I'd been secretive about Avery. I needed some serious help.

I'd spent the afternoon coming up with a three step plan to get things back on track.

Step one: Distance myself from Avery. I hoped that one day we could be friends again. However, I also needed to see the situation from Gwen's point of view—no more secrets.

Step two: Make a grand gesture to win back the girl. I had a few ideas but would need some help executing them.

I was going to have to ask for help from someone who most likely wanted nothing to do with me.

Step three: Start being a better human being in general, especially in my relationship with Sam.

"How are you holding up?" Sam asked as she entered my room. Speak of the devil. She'd made of habit of doing that the last few days, ever since I returned from the springs. She made herself comfortable on my bed while I seriously debated inviting her to move into my room. It would save her all the unnecessary walking. Plus, Luke's bed was already on the other wall. She could just use his and only move her clothing. Hell, she didn't even have to move her clothing. She could continue to get dressed in the other room preventing any awkward brother/sister moments. We could both benefit from the company of her spending more time over here. Or, at least I thought so.

"Why don't you ever sit on his bed?"

"What?"

"Luke's bed, you never sit on it. Only mine. Why is that?"

She lifted a shoulder. "I like your bed."

Because that explained it. I decided to get a jump on step three. "So, I was thinking about the road trip to San Diego."

"The one you said I wasn't allowed to come on and then never went yourself?"

"That would be it. Would you like try again? I think we might have missed our chance to visit Luke for the year, but maybe we could do something else. Oh," I exclaimed suddenly excited with the idea that popped into my head. "We could go take one with Luke this summer. It doesn't have to be anything long or anything."

"That sounds great."

"Yeah?" She didn't seem excited. Why didn't she sound excited?

"Yes, Mitch, it'll be fun. But right now, I'm starving. Wanna get a burger?"

I looked at her from the corner of my eye. She was not suggesting what I thought she was. "Where?" I asked suspiciously.

"Don't worry. I'm not a complete idiot. We can do fast food. I'll even treat."

"Why are you being nice to me?" I asked without making a move to get up.

"You're my brother. I love you even when you're an ass."

"I've been really selfish."

"Ugh." She flopped back on my mattress and gave me a look. "Mitch, I'm serious when I say I love you, but this melodramatic crap you have going on lately isn't very becoming. I miss you."

"I miss me too," I said giving my sister week smile. It was true. I felt like an entirely different person lately.

"Also, I heard some local band is playing at Wild Bill's."

"We're not twenty-one, no matter how much you will it into existence."

"It's teen night."

"Teen night," I said slowly. "At Wild Bill's?" I'd never been, but River Valley was a small town, and people talked. The bar had a strict 21 and up policy and was known for its rowdy atmosphere. The idea of it allowing underage kids in was unbelievable.

"I know, right? It turns out the drummer is the guy's nephew or something. I heard he pestered him until he agreed to do it on one of his slow nights. But if you don't wanna go..." Her voice trailed off in a song-like tone. She knew I couldn't resist. I wanted to see the place that had been the center of so many rumors.

"Fine. Let's go."

AFTER GRABBING SOME QUICK BURGERS, that were so weak compared to what I was used to, we drove to the bar. If I thought The Farmhouse was a hole in the wall, this place took it to a new level. The pavement was filled with potholes, and the neon sign proudly displayed *il Bill's*. Music blared from the building, so loudly we could hear it from the parking lot.

The guy at the door checked our IDs, gave us bright green wristbands, and drew black X's on both hands with a permanent marker. We weren't getting a drink tonight. Honestly, after the accident, I was reconsidering drinking at parties at all anymore. I didn't even want to think how much worse it would have been if I hadn't been sober.

Walking in, we could see the band on a makeshift stage. It consisted of a bunch of guys I recognized from high school. Like most people I knew, I wasn't close to any of them, but always on the peripheral of each other's groups. I'd never heard of their band, never knew these guys were in a band. After a few songs though, I could tell they practiced hard because they were pretty good.

The music was a mix of rock and folk music that bordered country. It was the best of the two worlds that dominated our small town. They played a few songs from the radio and a few songs I didn't recognize, songs I assumed were their originals.

I looked around, and I even spotted Avery directly in front of the small stage. She was cheering loudly at the end of every song and dancing enthusiastically while they played. I knew she was dating a guy in a band but never asked any more details. This must be them. She looked every bit in her element, and I was genuinely happy for her.

I also knew what I needed to do.

I waited until the band was done with their set to approach her. Sam ran over to a couple of friends from school giving me the perfect opportunity.

"Hey," I yelled over the crowd as I got closer.

"Mitch, I'm so glad you came," she said excitedly before giving me a hug. "Aren't these guys the best?"

"Yeah, they're great. What's their name?"

She laughed like I just said the most hilarious thing she'd ever heard. "They actually can't decide on a name. So they're just calling themselves The Band right now."

"The Band?"

"Yep." She rolled her eyes before looking around the bar. "Where's Gwen?"

"Pissed off."

"Oh, no. I thought you all had made up. What happened?"

"She read your text."

"Mitch." She closed her eyes. "I was afraid that might have been why you didn't respond. Did you tell her we were just friends?"

"Yeah. I just didn't tell her right away."

She punched me, and not very gently either. "You are such an idiot," she said, and hit me again.

"I know."

"Mitch. You have dragged that poor girl through the mud."

"I know," I yelled again.

"I bet if you apologize, she'll forgive you again," Avery suggested.

"I don't think she should."

"Maybe she will anyway. You guys belong together. Promise me you'll at least try, okay?"

"Okay, but I think that might mean we need to keep some distance between us. She thought she was the other woman."

She punched me again, and my arm was starting to get sore from the constant attack.

"Ouch." I rubbed the spot she'd just hit.

"You deserved that," she said, and pointed her finger at me. "But Mitch, I'm okay with space right now anyway. Carter and the guys are trying to get their band going, and I want to give them all the support I can."

"I'm sure they'll appreciate it."

"Yeah, I think they do. Good luck with Gwen," she said before giving me one last hug and walking off.

I looked over to where the guys were sitting, huddled close together drinking water from bottles. It hadn't escaped my attention that Carter, her new boyfriend, had been watching us the entire time. I was surprised he hadn't come over with all the hitting going on. I gave him a slight wave as Avery rushed back over to the band, which earned me a scowl.

I was striking out with the ladies. Even if I wanted to make the moves on someone, I was failing epically at every turn. I wanted to assure him Avery was safe from my advances, but I was too busy thinking of ways to win back my girl to bother.

CHAPTER TWENTY-THREE

GWEN

"STOP BOUNCING AROUND LIKE THAT. It's not like this is the first time you've done this. You should be happy you get to be here at all," my mother said across the park bench.

She had a last minute change of heart that I expected had more with getting to rub the entire situation in my face than actually showing compassion toward me. After my breakup with Mitch, I'd received a phone call from her. She told me about how she'd conveniently forgotten to cancel the tickets. It was better to go than to waste the money.

I told her how I conveniently never canceled my visit with Janet's family, so it worked out across the board.

Things weren't that easy though. We had a connecting flight, and the plane rides over were a disaster.

On the first flight, I sat between my mother and a man who felt entitled to use our shared armrest the entire flight. Not only that, his fat, hairy arm spilled into my personal space, making the already difficult trip unbearable.

The second flight, I struggled to keep my motion sickness at bay through extreme turbulence while my mother counted off the many ways I'd failed during the last couple of weeks.

Mitch was only the tip of the iceberg. I'd not spent enough time studying and moving in with Katie was a huge mistake. But in my mother's benevolence, I was still welcome to come home as soon as I admitted it was all a mistake.

I hated how trapped I was on the airplanes, how trapped I was on the hour drive that came after. I hated how trapped I was in our hotel room. And I definitely hated how trapped I felt sitting in the open air next to my mother as we waited for Janet to arrive.

I was completely over it.

"Did you hear what I just said, Gwendolyn?"

I looked up to see my mother's stern expression.

"I see them walking up. Try to control yourself while we're here."

My face spun in the direction of the parking lot just in time to see them walking up. Janet, who was so much bigger than I remembered, was being carried by her mom, Ally. Her dad, Michael, was right behind them.

Something was wrong though. Even from this distance, I could see Janet squirming around. She was crying about something, her face bright red from the exertion.

"No birfmom. No birfmom," she cried out as they got closer.

She was fighting to get as far away from me as possible. The tears started almost immediately. I'd done everything I could to get out here to see Janet. Listened to my mother and her lectures for this one moment, and she didn't want to see me. It was gut-wrenching.

I couldn't see Ally's face as she wrestled with Janet. She'd stopped walking and was whispering something in the girl's ear. I assumed it was something to get her to stop screaming long enough for our visit. I looked over to Michael who approached the table. His eyes were full of compassion. Not frustrated, not angry or put out. He looked at me like he knew how awful it must be for me at this moment. It took every bit of self-control not to run away.

"Hi, Gwen," he said before smiling at my mother. "Sorry about this. She missed her nap today, and you know how that is." Actually, I didn't know how that was. Not at all. "We know what an ordeal it is to come out here, so we didn't have the heart to cancel. I hate to say it, but this might not be a very good visit."

"That's okay," I said even though it was not okay. Not even a little.

We sat there awkwardly for a couple of minutes unsure of what to say. I could hear Ally speaking softly to Janet and caught bits and pieces of what she said. It was mostly things like "Don't you wanna see Birthmom Gwen?" and "She traveled very far to see you because you are so special."

From Janet, I mostly heard "No."

I didn't know what to do. It would be much easier for everyone to say don't worry about it and call it a day. But I felt like I needed to see her. I'd come all this way. I'd done everything I could to make this visit happen.

Eventually, the crying and screaming stopped.

Ally walked closer carrying Janet. My eyes went to where she was clutching her mother's shirt with both of her little hands. Her legs wrapped around her mom's waist and her head sat on Ally's shoulder.

"I'm sorry she's acting like this, she–"

"Didn't have her nap," I finished. "Your husband told us."

"Of course. I know you came all this way." Her words mirrored the ones that were spoken moments earlier, and her eyes were full of compassion.

"Hi, Janet," I said attempting to give my best smile, even as my heart felt like it was being ripped to shreds.

She buried her face against Ally's chest hiding from me as much as possible.

"I brought you something," I tried again pulling out a doll I bought a couple of days ago.

It was made by a local artist back in River Valley. A woman who made all kinds of crafts using wool. This particular doll was a mermaid with pink hair and a sewn on smile. I didn't know what three-year-old girls played with. I trusted that the lady who made it knew what she was talking about when she said Janet would like it. I had wanted to bring something special for her.

Janet eyed the doll suspiciously but didn't make a move to take it. I handed it to her mom who showed it to her. "Look what Birthmom Gwen brought you. Isn't she pretty? What a sweet gift."

She still didn't take it.

"How about we tell Birthmom about our day? Would you like that?" Ally said with a forced lightness. Like her husband, I could tell she was trying to make this visit work. "We made pancakes this morning."

"That sounds yummy," I said with the same false cheer.

Janet didn't say anything.

"Janet, what did we put in our pancakes?" Ally tried again.

"Fwoot," a quiet voice answered.

"I like fruit on my pancakes too—and whipped cream," I said.

At this, she turned to face me again. She still was cautious, and the smile she gave me was tentative at best. But at least she was acknowledging me.

It was the first time I'd gotten a good look at her since our visit started. She was beautiful. I got texts with pictures of her from time to time, but I hadn't seen her in person in a year. She'd changed so much. Her face was less chubby, more grown up. She had so many more teeth than she did in the picture I looked at daily, the one that was on my mirror at home from our last visit.

"Then what did we do, Janet?" her mom asked, attempting to get her to speak more.

The little girl in her arms looked down at her fingers. The nails were bright pink. I rarely painted my nails, mostly only my toes when summer rolled around. I desperately wished I had color on my nails to compare with hers.

"Did you paint your nails?"

A small nod.

"I think I need to paint my nails too."

Her little brow furrowed before she pushed her face against her mom again. So much for making headway. We all tried to bring her back into our conversation, but never gained more than a curious glance from Janet from that point on.

It was evident she felt safe with her parents. I just hated that Janet was afraid of me, that she felt the need to hide. I was the third wheel in this party, and it was killing me.

The visit dragged on slowly, and I watched as a look passed between her parents. "Gwen, we are so glad we could meet with you today, but I think it might be time to get this princess back home for a late nap," Ally said, as Michael grabbed Janet from her mother's arms.

"Say goodbye to Birthmom Gwen," her dad said, but she only snuggled against his chest harder. He gave me another sad smile before carrying her toward the car.

"I'm so sorry about how it went today," Ally explained, as the two walked away. "She's at this age where she's terrified of strangers."

Strangers.

Her eyes immediately widened when she realized what she said. I was the woman who carried Janet for nine months. My friends had alienated me and teased me. I spent my pregnancy researching my options and finding the perfect couple to adopt her. I had no doubt I chose the right people. The love they had for her was obvious.

But she was right. I loved Janet so much, but to her, I was a stranger. I was the lady she saw once a year. She didn't know what the word birthmom meant. It wasn't fair for me to put that kind of pressure on her, to expect her to love me the same way I loved her.

Tears came quickly for the second time in our visit. It wasn't a violent sob or a noisy, heaving cry. No, it was a constant stream of silent tears because I knew what was coming next. I knew it was what was best for everyone, at least for now. I didn't want to say the words that were coming.

"Ally, today was hard and–"

"Gwen," she interrupted gently, but I kept going.

"I am so glad I chose you and your husband. You both love her so much. But I can also see this is hard for her. She doesn't understand what's going on and I'm a stranger."

"I didn't mean it like that."

"I know, but it's true." I took a deep breath to steady my

voice. "I still want the updates you send. I don't want to lose those, but I think it will be best for her if we didn't do these visits for a while. When you're ready and when she's ready, I want to come back and see her. I'll want to get to know her," I finished, as my voice finally cracked. I'd made it through my speech, and I couldn't say anything else.

"Oh, Gwen," she said, and pulled me into a hug. "You have given us a gift. One we are thankful for every day. We would be more than happy to send you updates. And know that we will be glad to restart visits whenever you want to."

"Thank you," I whispered before we broke away from the embrace.

She gave my mom a hug before walking to the car where her husband and daughter were waiting. Stopping at the car, she gave us one last look before getting in and driving off. As soon as the car turned the corner, I let the reality of everything sink in. I broke down in the park, uncaring of any audience we may have gathered.

It was the right thing to do, and I knew that. But it was the hardest thing I'd ever experienced, second only to when Janet went home with her parents from the hospital.

"I'm so proud of you," I heard my mom say. Her hand was rubbing soothing circles on my back. "Let's go home."

MY MOM HAD BEEN INCREDIBLY SWEET the entire journey home. From letting me sit in the window seat of our flight to getting me copious amounts of chocolate in the form of candy and mochas.

She didn't say much, which was the biggest blessing of all. There was no criticism, no lecture, no empty platitudes. It looked like I wasn't the only one who was drastically moved by our time in California. But neither one of us was ready to voice our thoughts on what had happened. It was better that way.

I wasn't sure what this meant for my future relationship with Janet. I wasn't sure what it meant for my current relationship with my mom. My brain couldn't focus on any of it. I was only trying to keep one foot in front of the other, so to speak, until I got home and could finally crash for the remaining days of spring break.

So when my mom drove up to mine and Katie's place, I had a hard time processing the extra vehicle out front. What the hell was Mitch's SUV doing parked out front next to Katie's? I couldn't deal with anything else right now.

Walking through the front door was just as strange. Mitch and Katie sat together on the couch in deep conversation with one another. When they noticed my entrance, Mitch immediately stood up and walked to me. He stopped short, just inches from me, almost as if he'd just remembered we were fighting. Katie sat unmoving on the couch pretending not to watch what was unfolding before her.

"Gwen," he whispered quietly, pulling my attention back to the boy who stood so, so close. A thousand unspoken words were behind the word. I could see it in his eyes. He must have seen my reply in my own because he opened his arms just as I moved toward him.

His embrace was everything I needed.

I couldn't figure it all out today. But I could take what he was offering.

We went to my room, and Mitch stayed with me the rest of the night, never pushing for more than the embrace. He didn't ask me about my trip, didn't apologize for what had happened before. He somehow knew better than to interrupt the silence.

After lying together for a couple of hours, I finally spoke. "I'm not going back."

"To California?" he asked, and I nodded. "Why not?"

"Mitch, I love her. But it's time for me to let her go."

"Okay," he said, and pulled me closer. "Okay."

He didn't say anything else. I didn't say anything else. Because really, what *was* there to say?

CHAPTER TWENTY-FOUR

MITCH

GWEN BROKE my heart the night before with her crying. When I woke up the next morning on her pallet bed, she was gone. I hadn't even noticed her getting up. Crawling off the floor, I walked out to the living room to find Julian and Katie sitting on the couch watching television.

"She went to her mom's," Katie answered my unspoken questions. "I don't know how long she'll be there, but if you want to do this, we'd better act now."

I pulled out my phone to look at the time. It was much later than I realized, which meant I slept in. Crap. It was okay though. We could still make this work. "Is everything out back?"

"Yep, and thankfully Gwen didn't look out back before she left."

"She doesn't look so good," Julian said. "Maybe we shouldn't be thankful she's too depressed to look outside?"

"You know what I meant," Katie said as she got up, but I couldn't help but agree with Julian.

We all went out back to where our supplies were waiting. I'd bought most of them the day before, everything except for the biggest, most necessary item.

"I still can't believe you bought a refrigerator for him," Julian grumbled from his spot in the yard. The ground was free of snow, but it was still cold as hell. He'd begun cutting large squares from Styrofoam while Katie got to work opening the paint for the giant cardboard box.

"Well, technically I bought your mom a fridge," Katie countered with a smile. She was wrapped up in a thick jacket.

"Which she appreciates more than you realize. This just seems over the top."

"It *is* over the top. That's why I love it. Also, I'm happy your mom got to benefit from it." She lifted her shoulder. "Her old one was ancient."

I watched their exchange wondering, not for the first time, just how much money Katie had. When I approached her with my idea, she jumped on board without a second thought. Together we came up with a plan that I hoped like hell would work.

"I love you," he said sounding grumpy, but I could tell there was devotion behind the words.

"I love you too. Now stop complaining and keep painting," she teased with a wink at her boyfriend.

I looked down at my project. My phone displayed an article giving detailed instructions for turning a package of markers into a device that I hoped would make Gwen smile. It involved taking them apart and putting them back together in a completely different way. I had super glue, electrical tape, and paint. I was feeling strangely crafty.

"Mitch, you've been on my naughty list for the better part of a month," Katie said, looking up at me, but not stopping her work.

"I know."

"But I think this is one of the most romantic gestures you could do for her. I hope it works."

"Me too," I answered quietly. "Your blanket inspired me, you know?"

"My blanket? Oh, I'm going to kill Gwen for telling you about that."

"It was very romantic. Or at least that's what Gwen keeps telling me. What do you think, Julian?" I asked.

"It was something else," he answered.

I'd been struggling with what I could do to win Gwen back. The road trip to see Janet was supposed to be my big gift. When I screwed that up, I knew it would be hard to top.

"Well, I think this is great," Katie encouraged.

"Last attempt to show her how much I care." I shrugged, still working on my gadget. I shoved a small battery operated light on one end of the marker before wrapping electrical tape around the entire thing.

"Don't screw up again," Julian said, as he used his knife to cut another section out. The effect was quite menacing. When Katie shot him an appalled looked, he continued. "I'm serious. We all care about Gwen. She's amazing, and I think you're good for her, Mitch. But I also don't want to see you hurt her again. She doesn't deserve it."

It was the most Julian had said about the situation. He gave his help reluctantly, and I knew that. And I was sure it was only because Katie pushed him.

"I know, man. I'm literally attempting to go back in time here."

Katie laughed at that. She laughed while I held my breath.

Katie thought I was being cute. She thought I was being

romantic. I didn't think she realized how much of my future was on the line. It sounded dramatic when I thought of it that way. We were freshmen in college, not even old enough to legally drink yet. That said, I couldn't imagine a future without Gwen. She was my best friend and the girl I wanted to spend forever with.

I went back to work with a renewed fervor in an attempt to make everything as perfect as I could. I would look up occasionally to see where Julian and Katie were, but mostly I stayed focused on my task.

What seemed like only minutes later, Gwen got back. Since we were outside, and we were all quietly working, we heard her car as soon as it pulled up. I looked up at Katie as my heart felt like it was beating out of my chest.

The paint was still slightly wet, and some of the details never made it onto the box, but it would have to do. I ran inside to get dressed while Julian and Katie ran quick interference.

I sent up a silent prayer this would work.

CHAPTER TWENTY-FIVE

GWEN

I STILL WASN'T sure what to think about my morning with my mother.

She'd expected things to go back to normal after our trip to California. I had experienced enough whiplash these last few weeks to last me a lifetime. Part of me wanted to run back to my mom and forget everything that had happened. The other part of me screamed at my heart to be more cautious.

I was willing to forgive her. That didn't mean I was loading my possessions up to move back in with her and Dad. I was learning forgiveness didn't mean that things were sunshine and rainbows. It didn't mean that you acted like those horrible things never happened. I would guard my heart. I would be careful with my choices.

When I pulled up to the house I shared with Katie, I wondered if Mitch would still be inside. That was another area of my life I needed to sort out like nobody's business. I didn't overthink it when I let him hold me the night before. We didn't discuss whether or not he was here to stay this time.

I wasn't sure what I wanted this time.

When I got to the front door, I pulled out my key only to have Katie open it before I got a chance. She looked giddy while Julian stood behind her looking as disgruntled as ever.

"Um, hey guys," I said, confused by the welcome committee before me.

"How was your mom's?" Katie asked, still with a goofy grin on her face.

"Exhausting," I admitted. I was looking forward to my bed, still unsure if I wanted Mitch to be there or not.

"So you'll probably want this banana then," Katie giggled. I looked over just in time to see Julian rolling his eyes. What the hell was going on? "You should always bring a banana to a party."

It was an obvious Doctor Who reference, but I couldn't figure out why she looked like she just saw a baby koala bear or something.

"Tell me there isn't a party inside," I said as I went up on my toes to peek inside our house before she could answer me.

The lights were on, so I could easily see there wasn't any surprise celebration waiting for me.

Thank goodness.

"No party," Katie answered anyway, handing me the fruit she'd been holding.

"Okay," I said slowly. "So can I come in then? It's freezing out here."

"Oh, right," she said and moved out of the way. "Actually, Julian and I were just on our way out. We'll see you later."

"Okay," I repeated as I watched them walk quickly toward Katie's SUV.

Julian gave me one last look before getting in. He lifted

his brows and mouthed good luck to me. I was thoroughly confused but closed the door. I set my keys and purse down on the table and looked at the banana in my hands.

I loved my friend, but she was acting weird. Or at least that's what I thought until I saw what was written on the fruit I held.

Go out back.

I didn't go out back. Instead, I looked out the window into the yard. I wanted to laugh. I wanted to cry. What I ended up doing was making some weird noise that didn't sound like either.

I opened the door and walked out to see Mitch standing next to what looked like a giant cardboard box turned into TARDIS. It was taller than both of us and painted bright blue. It even had cutouts on it to make it look like the famous time-traveling phone booth.

When I looked back to Mitch, I noticed he wore a long jacket and colorful striped scarf. He looked like the fourth Doctor. When he lifted an end of the scarf and swung it around, I smiled.

"I wish I could say I knitted it myself."

My smile turned into a laugh. "No, you don't. It takes way too long."

"Almost as long as this scarf. I mean, seriously, I think there's enough for both of us."

"Probably."

"Want to find out?" he asked, his expression hopeful. I wanted to run to him but remembered the promise I made to myself earlier. I needed to be more cautious in my relationships, especially with Mitch. He'd hurt me time and time again.

"I don't know."

"Please, Gwen. Just hear me out. After I finish, if you want me to leave, I will."

"Okay." I sighed and walked closer. When I did, I could see Mitch had a homemade sonic screwdriver in his hand. It even had a light on the end.

"Are you impressed?" he asked waggling his eyebrows at me. "Didn't realize I was so handy, did you?" I pushed him playfully feeling a little like my old self.

"Whoa, Gwen. I said handy, not handsy. Stop making me feel like a piece of meat." He stood up straight and grabbed the lapels of his jacket. "Besides, I've got people to save and don't have time for that right now."

"Oh, really?"

"Yes, really. It's just one of the many responsibilities of a Time Lord. Now come on, you can be my companion," he said dragging me into the cardboard box. Once we both squeezed in and he pulled the cutout door shut he whispered to me, "It's not bigger on the inside."

I laughed again. "No, it's not."

"But it's more romantic this way."

"Assuming we both brushed our teeth, at least," I said, quickly thinking back to what I ate earlier and hoped it wasn't something smelly.

He leaned closer. "You don't mind that I used yours, right?"

"Gross," I said pushing him. His back hit the side of the box, and it moved slightly.

"Careful," he said steadying himself and wrapped one of his arms around me. He was so close. "I don't know how sturdy this phone booth is."

"I think it's cardboard," I whispered.

"What?" he gasped. "I thought it was the genuine TARDIS."

"Aw, poor Mitch. You got swindled," I teased and looked around the inside of the box. "So, what is all this?"

"I thought you'd never ask," he said loosening his arm and lifting the sonic screwdriver between us. "Do you remember when I asked you about what superpower you wanted?"

"I said time travel." Everything began clicking into place.

"Ta-da," he said and raised his hands as much as our current confines would allow.

"Mitch, when I said–"

"Please," he interrupted. "Can we please start over? Can we go back to that day when we almost kissed in my truck after the movie? Or, to right after the accident? I'd scoop you up in my arms because I'd just be so grateful we were all okay. Hell, I'd even settle for the coffee we had the next day so that I didn't start this downward spiral we've been on for the last few weeks."

"When I said I wanted to go back in time, it was before any of that. I was running from my past," I reminded him. "But I'm not running anymore. I've found peace with my decision that should have been there all along. Even with my most recent visit, I feel closure that has always been missing."

"I'm happy for you, Gwen. I am. But I need to know if there's room for me in your life. Tell me I'm not just another thing to come to terms with in your past," he pleaded. "Please, tell me I'm in your future."

I listened to his words trying to process it all. I stood quietly making my decision. Did I want him in my future?

"There's only one way to find out," I finally answered.

"Give me another chance?"

"No, you idiot. We're in a time-machine. Let's go see."

Mitch's smile widened and those dimples I'd missed so much appeared. They'd been there all along, of course, but there was something so special about seeing them with his patented smile that made me happy.

"I have no idea how to work this thing," he stage-whispered in my ear, so I did the only thing I could. I pressed my fingertips against the wall of the box and made a lot of beep-boop noises. I heard Mitch's chuckle from beside me.

I started to move back and forth like we were traveling through time and space. It was something the Doctor and his companion always did on the show. Unfortunately, I got carried away and bumped into Mitch hard. We hit the opposite side of the box and sent it crashing to the ground.

I fell on top of him, and we both started laughing hysterically.

"Oh, my gosh. We are the coolest people I know," I managed to say while gasping for air.

"And you are the most graceful girl I know."

"It's true," I said smiling but refused to move from my spot on top of him.

"So how far in the future did you take us anyway? Should we see if we end up together?"

"It doesn't matter."

"It doesn't?" he asked, suddenly serious.

"Nope, because I know it includes you. Today, tomorrow, whenever," I answered.

Then I kissed him because it was true. Things might not always be easy. They weren't easy now. But I knew I always wanted Mitch by my side.

LET'S KEEP IN TOUCH!

 Kayla has loved to read as long as she can remember. While she started out reading spooky stories that had her hiding under her covers, she now prefers stories with a bit more kissing.

When she gets a chance to watch TV, she enjoys cheesy sci-fi and super-hero shows.

Most days, you'll catch her burning dinner in an attempt to cook while reading just *one* more chapter.

Kayla lives in the sunshine state with her husband and three boys.

Find me online:
www.tirrellblewrites.com

ALSO BY KAYLA TIRRELL

Varsity Girlfriends:

Courtside Crush

Game Plan

Shelfbrooke Academy:

Tessa

Boys of Summer:

Beauty and the Beach

Mountain Creek Drive:

Chasing Love

Carnival Wishes

River Valley Lost & Found:

All The Things We Lost

All The Things We Found

All The Things We Were

Collection of Sweet Shorts:

Home For Christmas

The Art of Taking Chances

Disastrous Dates:

Disastrous Dates: The Complete Series

Children's Chapter Book:

Help! My Parents Are Zombies!

CPSIA information can be obtained
at www.ICGtesting.com
Printed in the USA
LVHW080028170920
666293LV00014B/367

9 781973 853916